A SEMI
True Story

REV. DR. KENNETH D. LINNELL OSL

Copyright © 2024 Rev. Dr. Kenneth D. Linnell OSL.

All rights reserved. No part of this book may be reproduced, stored, or transmitted by any means—whether auditory, graphic, mechanical, or electronic—without written permission of both publisher and author, except in the case of brief excerpts used in critical articles and reviews. Unauthorized reproduction of any part of this work is illegal and is punishable by law.

ISBN: 979-8-89031-949-4 (sc)
ISBN: 979-8-89031-950-0 (hc)
ISBN: 979-8-89031-951-7 (e)

Because of the dynamic nature of the Internet, any web addresses or links contained in this book may have changed since publication and may no longer be valid. The views expressed in this work are solely those of the author and do not necessarily reflect the views of the publisher, and the publisher hereby disclaims any responsibility for them.

One Galleria Blvd., Suite 1900, Metairie, LA 70001
(504) 702-6708

DEDICATION

I dedicate this collection of thoughts to my one and only daughter in law Fran, without who's support and encouragement this collection of memories would never have come together in one place let alone have been written down.

Thanks Fran, with love Dad.

CONTENTS

Authors Note vii
Preface ix

Part I: A Place to Start 1
Memories 3
1945 6
Idaho 12
Kansas 15
California 18
Kansas Once Again 23
Idaho Summer 26
Additional Memories and thoughts of Idaho 30

Part I.b: Some Over Laps 37
Semi Adulthood 39
First Jobs Away from the Farm 40
Kansas for the Last time 51

Part II: Adulthood 55
Military Service and Girls 57
September 3, 1957 the US Air Force for real! 59
Chennault Air Force Base, Lake Charles, LA 61
Air Police 64
A memory or two of Thule 75

Part II.a: Adulthood on Hold 87
Education (better late than never) 89
Grandmothers 93

Part II.b: Children 103
The Son 105
Daughter #1 109
Daughter #2 112
Daughter #3 118

Part II.c: Adulthood Resumed 121

Part III: The Rest of the Story 125
Awakening 127
Religion 130
A Brief Pause 134
The Guide 136
August 19, 1979 137
Life on the edge of a two edged sword 143

Part IV: The Rest of the Story – A Final Word 149
August, 1, 1984 151

AUTHORS NOTE

For a long period of time this work remained as "Untitled". I had no idea what to call this collection of memories and thoughts. Then one day I was listening to my favorite author, poet, singer, and theologian, Jimmy Buffet, as he sang a song entitled "A Semi True Story".

As I listened, I realized the song was a memoir or biography of sorts, and Jimmy was saying as we remember events, we change details by embellishment or by cleaning them up a little, and thus even while based in fact, truth, and lives lived, they become "Semi True."

The chorus to this magical song includes these words:

> "It's a semi-true story, believe it or not
> I made up a few things and there's some I forgot
> But the life and the telling are both real to me
> And they all run together and turn out to be
> A semi-true story"

Jimmy has gone on before us to that placed promised, and he is greatly missed. I hope he smiles if he realizes I have co-opted his title for this work. His work and the record he has left, is a treasure full of jewels and gems waiting for us to use.

He is this author's favorite artist, singer, poet and theologian. Thanks Jimmy!

PREFACE

I began this effort some time ago as a series of loosely related gatherings of memories of a life lived as most of us live our lives. We all, I believe, conduct our journey through life by simply placing one foot in front of the other, moving forward towards a future we conceive in our minds. We do this while being firmly planted and inexplicably tied to the present moment as each foot is lifted and moved into the unknown moment of a future which instantaneously becomes the present as the foot touches its destination.

This sounds like a rather dull existence, however, the reality is, because of the unknown never certain nature of the future life as we know it, it is one filled with adventure, expectation, disappointment laughter, joy, sorrow, and every emotion known to our species.

Mostly we spend a large amount of our time in memories of the events of our lives. It is these memories that truly effect our present and the hope of our futures.

It is these memories, particularly the memories of one life not yet completed, that are to be explored in these pages. Also there are accompanying thoughts which hopefully connect the memories, giving them meaning through the explanation and reasoning of those thoughts.

The memories to be explored are of an ordinary life. Not one that has soared in to the highs of societal prominence, but of just an ordinary person who simply kept putting one foot in front of the other, because that was the best choice, all the while making choices in the direction given that foot. Choices, made based upon the hopes and dreams glimpsed through the veil of the forever moving and unattainable future.

This is also a recollection of a faith journey and the eventual realization that the traveler is never alone on this journey, but is always and forever guided and prompted by an ever present force known by many names throughout the human realm. This Guide is always there prompting and presenting the direction for that foot to go, yet it is our choice to accept or not. It is that choice, I believe, that creates the memories and determines whether they are memories of joy, sorrow, success, or failure.

Some of this retelling may over lap and for that I beg the readers indulgence. I also tell the story in the third person, referring to myself as "the Boy".

I also would point out that the life recounted here is of consequence only to my family and close friends. However, I tell this story in the belief that all of our stories are of significance and consequence. So if my story and memories are worth the telling, so are those of the reader.

The Aborigines of Australia believe it is the knowing and the telling of the stories of their people which connects them to the community and the land of their ancestors and their present. It is also their belief, it is the stories and their continuous telling that gives the person, family, community, and ultimately the world, even the universe substance.

I believe they are very correct. I also believe, our stories regardless of their supposed insignificance, are necessary for our descendants to know who they are. It is the stories of their people, as much or even more than their DNA which shapes who they are and who they become. Therefore, I am attempting to write my story for two reasons:

First, I write so that my decedents will know their story so that they might know from where they have come. I also write for my children, so that with a small amount of knowledge might also come a small amount of forgiveness.

Second, It is my hope that the reader might realize in the reading of my story, that theirs is also worth the telling.

It is hoped that stories left untold for whatever reason, will be seen as significant and be told. For it is the belief of this author that it is our stories which connect us all and cause us to be connected to the human community. It is believed it is the stories which form the community, making every story a most precious thing.

A priceless thing which is meant to be shared, which if lost should be and must be mourned with great fervor.

PART I

A Place to Start

MEMORIES

Memories are strange things. It is written somewhere that ones memories are affected by the moment one selects them for review. This is, last in, first out. Supposedly they are also changed each and every time they are retrieved, This maybe true, yet, experience has shown some memories never change. They remain the same regardless of how many reviews are made, and remain impervious to the wishes and desires for them to be different just once. It would appear change depends on the importance or impact of a particular event on the matrix of life. Strong impact, no change occurs in the memory, it becomes engraved in stone. Little impact, invites changes or short lived memories, and so on.

All this is reviewed simply to preface my memories as the eldest of the three boys who spent the summer of Nineteen Hundred Fifty playing together in the tall blue grass and white clover of an Idaho summer, as I recall their story. The memories are now seventy three plus years old, yet remain as fresh and unchanged as at the moment of occurrence.

∞

The boy's earliest memories are like those of most of us.

He recalls a sunlit day and a journey trough the country side. Fields of grain, green and waving in the soft breeze. The journey is with father, mother and sister Clara in her basket. They are in an old car. A black one as he remembers.

Mother and father are laughing, obviously enjoying each other and the journey trough the country side of North West Kansas.

It must be stated here that at the time the boy did not know it was North West Kansas, but that this knowledge came at a later stage in life.

Suddenly the side of the car where sister Clara was riding in her basket, fell and began to drag on the ground. At the same moment the boy saw the wheel of the car roll past the car and into the field and disappear into the tall green grain. He remembers father saying something loud and mother bursting into loud laughter. Father chasing after the wheel and then doing something at the side of the old car. While father chased the wheel, mother got sister Clara and the boy out of the car, and they moved to the edge of the field and watched father, as he put the wheel back on the car.

This particular memory ends here. There is no recollection of the remainder of that journey.

It is also the only remaining memory of sister Clara, as she died shortly after this moment in memory. The boy was just past his second birthday.

⁂

The next indelible memories are of a big house on a wide street in Goodland, Kansas. Memories of father and mother laughing a lot. Staying over night across the street because the big house had to be fumigated (big word for a young mind).

Traveling to a place called St. Francis to visit with fathers younger sister, Virgey, and her family.

Standing on the street, with father holding his hand, as father talked to another man. He remembers looking up at father and this other man, seeing them so tall they seemed to grow right into the sky. The man father was talking with, reached down from this great height and patted the boy on the head. How could he reach down that far, he remembers thinking to himself. He remembers the exact spot on the street in Goodland, Kansas, where this moment in time occurred. In later years he often stood on that same spot, and remembered father. He could do that once more, if the street in Goodland has not been altered over the passing of time.

Strongest of all is Christmas 1944.

That morning is filled with happiness. Mother and father were busy talking, laughing, and doing the thing that grown ups do on Christmas morning. The boy and baby brother were there. Baby brother wasn't doing much, after all he hadn't been here very long. He was still pretty much a wiggling pink worm as far as the boy was concerned.

The boy was busy doing his favorite morning things. Because Christmas day came on Monday that year, and father had to be gone on his job as a fireman for the Rock Island railroad on Monday, the family had Christmas on Sunday, or Christmas eve.

Because of this the boys memories of that Christmas contain two of his favorite things in the whole word at that time in his four and a half year old life. The colored funnies in the Rocky Mountain News and Christmas presents.

Remember it was the years of World War II and most four year old boys who got presents, got a doll dressed as a military person of some type. The boy's was an Army Airborne Sargent all dressed up in full uniform, complete with stripes on his arm an a parachute pack on his back.

The Boy had just finished reading, actually looking at the pictures, while father read the story, printed in the funnies. His favorite was "Terry and the Pirates". Today's episode had been about a volcano, a mountain that smoked, and someone getting tossed into the volcano. The boys favorite character was "Smiling Jack". So the Army Sargent Parachute doll became known as Smiling Jack. An upturned box became the volcano and Smiling jack parachuted into the volcano time after time to rescue someone.

All Christmas memories should be so resplendently remembered.

1945

(The events are true, they happened. Yet, these events had small effect on a world in the final months of a war that had made truly indelible memories for thousands. None the less they remain and are etched into the mind of those whose threads of life drew them through these events.)

It is a cold dark night on the northwestern Kansas plains. It is January 20, 1945. The war in Europe is in its final months, as is the war in the Pacific. The small Kansas town sitting comfortably on this cold prairie has grown accustomed to knocks on the door in the middle of the night, and the terror of those within, as they greet the messenger standing at the door with drooping countenance, holding the telegram.

But this night is different.

The knock on the door is accompanied by the wailing moan of train whistles on every steam engine currently located at the Rock Island Railroad round house and rail yard. The screaming whistles are blasting continuously, Three long blasts and silence, then three long blasts over and over and over. Everyone in this small northwestern Kansas town knows the meaning of this steam driven terror as it invades the peace of their sleep. As it turns the warmth of sleep into the cold chill of terror.

Somewhere in the dark of that cold night there is a train wreak, and judging by the volume and length of this signal, a bad one. Every man in town, who works for the Rock Island, hurriedly left the comfort of homes, covered in their denim uniform of overalls and blanket lined denim coat and denim railroaders cap. They hurried to the rail yard to begin the recovery of what they knew by experience was the beginning of a long night and day as they cleared the wreck from the rails.

All hoped that none of their friends doors would be knocked upon that night. Others waited holding their breath, waiting for the knock on their door which would bring the news that their world had been changed forever.

A moment of their lives made indelible in memory forever.

Awakened by the whistles and the knocking at the door the boy stood on the top landing, of the stairs to the floor where he and his brother slept. Too short to see over the banister, he looked, he watched through the balusters as mother slowly opened the door. She stood shaking as the man on the other side of the threshold said words that could not be understood by the young ears listening so far away, across the room, and half way up the wall.

The man had brought the word. The wreck was indeed bad. The young boy soon knew his mothers husband and best friend, his and his brother's father was gone. The first to leave, never to return.

⁓∞⁓

The day had been long and the boy was worn beyond wakefulness. He slept on the old worn sofa. Surrounded by the smells of years of embedded dust and constant use. Mother and her sister sat at the table a few feet away in the dining area. He dosed in the comfort of the hushed sound of their voices in earnest conversation.

Suddenly he heard father calling his name. Once, twice, three times. The boy even in his extreme youth was frightened, because he had spent that day among adults as they buried his fathers body. Even at the extreme old age of four and one half years, the boy knew this should not be.

He had a vivid image of his fathers body asleep, surrounded by flowers. He did not wake up even though there were a lot of adults around him, talking about him. The boy knew he was dead. He understood the meaning of that word. It was a constant in the lives of the people who lived during the years of the war. Even the youngest of the young came to the knowledge of death during those years.

He quickly turned and standing there in front of him was his father reaching out, calling his name. Just as quickly, in fright, he turned in a rolling lurch, burying his face into the old sofa between the back and the cushions. The smell remains to this day. The musty dust filled smell of old velour. Even the color remains indelible, brown, the golden brown of a bear caught in a moment of sunshine.

After a time, unknown in duration, yet for the four and a half year old mind it seemed, and is remembered as an eternity, the boy turned back. No longer afraid, anxious to speak to his father one more time. Anxious to know what he had to say. Anxious to know what was so important that a return from burying was needed.

All this is the words of the now eighty three year old mind of the boy. At that moment all he knew was that he had the chance to speak to the father he loved so much one more time. But, he was gone, never again to be seen or heard. The boy learned at that moment the hurt and disappointment of missed opportunity. Also the tragedy of a faint heart.

Many events took place during the weeks and months following that cold January night. Yet none were strong enough to leave a lasting impression in the almost five year old mind of the boy. Also no memories during that time of his brother exist. Middle brother was there on that night in his crib, but not yet important enough to make an indelible impression. The youngest brother was also there, but in his mothers womb, destined to make his appearance on Valentines day 1945. All three boys were there as witness, the night of their fathers death, but only the oldest ever had memories of that event.

This is mother. The picture was taken shortly before fathers death in January of 1945

The car traveled down the roadway. To call it a highway by the standards of so many years into the future, would certainly be misleading in the least. Yet in its day U. S. Highway 30 was a major artery across the northern portion of the United States. It was a happy time. Mother and the three boys together. No distractions. Mother was, or seemed to her young brood, happy. At least she smiled now and then and her eyes and cheeks were not covered with tears as often any more. The sun shone brightly through the windows of the old car. There is no memory of what kind of car, only that it was old. Occasionally a large truck would pass them on the long flat, straight highway. All, according to memory were silver streaks as they passed by fast and close. On their silver sides and back were three big red letters P.I.E.

As each would pass, the oldest would sing out, " There goes our money!" Brother would clap his little hands and laugh. It was a grand game. The oldest had overheard the big people talking to mother and what he had heard was that money was being sent ahead to be there when the young brood and their mother arrived at their destination, IDAHO.

However, the brothers had decided that only the big trucks, with the big red letters, P.I.E. on their sides and backs were important enough to carry mothers money. After all, P.I.E. spelled money to their young minds.

Memories, strange beings they are indeed.

∞

Night. Through sleep filled eyes, peeping cautiously up over the car door edge, through the dust covered window. The boy saw bright lights and people milling around. Mother was standing with a man doing something at the side of the car. She had done this often during this journey away from Kansas, toward this magical place called Idaho. Mother had told the boy, when he asked what she was doing, that she was filling the tank with gasoline. Why she needed to do that he did not know, but if mother thought it necessary, then it was necessary. Mother smiled more the farther the car took them from Kansas, so if she wanted to fill the tank with gasoline it was all right with him.

He heard mother ask a man where they were, "Little America, Wyoming," the voice replied. Mother got in the car and started to leave this place called "Little America, Wyoming. The boy wide awake now, watched as she guided the car away from the bright lights and toward the dark road.

In the headlights standing by the side of the road was a man. He was dressed in strange clothes, all the same color. Almost the same color as the old sofa left behind in the house in Kansas, but different. On his arms were stripes and patches. On the front of his jacket were strange colored bars, all pressed closely together in rows.

Mother stopped the car in front of the strangely dressed man. "Where you going Soldier?" the boy heard mother ask. "Idaho." the boy heard the man mother called Soldier say. Strange mother had never mentioned anyone else going to IDAHO. "So are we," mother replied, "If you drive, so I can rest, you can go with us." "Yes Mam. I'd be glad too," Soldier replied as he moved toward the car. Mother picked up baby brother and slid over to the opposite side of the car as Soldier got in. Soldier made the car move toward the highway and once more they were off to Idaho.

IDAHO. A magical place where silver trucks with big red letters on their sides and backs take money, and people called Soldier go. A magical place that makes mother smile as she sleeps with little brother in her arms, while soldier makes the car move on down the road.

IDAHO

Ooh! Idaho was a wonderful place! At least for a preschool mind. The boy played in the sun. Roamed the field next to the pale blue house on the road next to the canal. The field was covered with soft blue green alfalfa, at least that's what mother said. Mother said they fed it to cows. Strange wonderful place this Idaho.

There was a tree next to the fence in the field where the alfalfa grew. It was a wonderful tree! It had leaves covered with a soft silvery fuzz and when the breeze moved the leaves, they sparkled like the new dime the boy had in his pocket. When the leaves sparkled he would take the dime out of his pocket and look at it, careful not to drop it. The boy loved his dime tree and the dime he kept in his pocket. Mother had given him the dime. Mother smiled most of the time now.

∞

A new house. The boy didn't like this house much. The outside was not as pretty as the house beside the alfalfa field. There was no canal or dime tree either. There was only a large dusty yard and a big old musty barn, that mother's friend said the boy couldn't go into. The boy didn't like mothers friend very much.

There was a big field that grew nothing but grass, in this field were cows, they ate grass not alfalfa. There were horses too, the boy didn't know what they ate. They just ran around the field a lot. Sometimes when mother's friend was gone, the boy, mother and brother would have to go into the field and "shoo" the horses back into the barn. "Shoo", that's what mother called it. Horses are strange. Mother doesn't like horses very much.

Mother's friend and mother are talking very loud. Mother is crying and her friend is hollering at her. Mother hollers at the boy once in a while. The friend is picking up a big square knife thing mother uses to chop up chickens. Now he is chasing mother around the room waving the big knife thing at her. He pushes her up against the wall and chops the wall above her head. Mother hollers at the boy to run and he does. He runs to the open window and jumps through it, landing in the bushes outside. He lays there listening to the chopping on the wall. He is very still and very quiet. Mother finds him, she is not crying any more and she does not smile.

Indelible.

⁂

The sun is shining brightly as the boy and his friends walk down the street and turn into the corner drug store. It is a dark red brick building on the corner of the street in a small Idaho town. Mother and the three boys moved here not long after he jumped through the window. Mother still doesn't smile as much as she used to.

The boy and his friends walk over to the big cooler, that's what mother calls it, and reach in. Each one helps themselves to a Popsicle and walks back out on to the sidewalk. They don't pay, mother owns the drug store on the corner of this small Idaho town called Kuna.

Baby brother is sick most of the time. The boy doesn't remember much of him except that mother called his sickness, "Rheumatic fever'. The boy and his other brother spend a lot of time together. Often when they are outdoors, that's what mother calls outside, they look up and watch as very big airplanes fly over them. Mother say's the war thing has been over for a while now and the army guys are coming home. The brothers wonder if their uncle is on one of those planes flying over them.

When mother isn't working in the drug store, she's taking care of baby brother. The boy doesn't think baby brother is worth much. He heard the women who takes care of baby brother, when mother is in the drug store, call baby brother, "a pruny little bastard!" The boy thinks that fits pretty good because he is pruny.

Mother doesn't smile at all any more.

Mother and her boys 1945-46 Taken while the family lived in Kuna, Idaho. Of course Mother in the background. The Boy on the left, brother Bob on the right and brother Bill in the center. You can see he is "pruny".

KANSAS

There are no memories of how they got there, but, here the brothers are in Kansas once more. Uncle Bo, must have been on one of those big planes that passed overhead, at the drug store in that small Idaho town. He is here now. He and the boys are living in a different house in that same small Kansas town. The town where they used to live with father and mother. The one where father left them and never came back. Mother is also gone now.

They are alone in a house filled with strangers called aunts and uncles, and a grandma and a grandpa. Grandpa is sick and hollers at them from a bedroom, to quit making noise. He doesn't have a big square knife thing that chops up chickens, so they ignore him.

The two older brothers don't like it in Kansas much. There are too many people in the house. They don't get to play much. They have to do things called, chores, dry dishes, sweep the kitchen floor and weed the garden. Weeding the garden is not too bad, at least it's outside. Baby brother doesn't have to do anything.

The aunts, the boys can't understand why they call them,"aunts". They don't look anything like the little bug things that crawl around the yard. Anyway, the aunts play with baby brother all the time, like he is some kind of doll or something. But he is still pruny.

What ever happened to mother and how did they wind up in Kansas again, is something the older two brothers ask each other often. Baby brother is too useless and pruney to matter,

One of the aunts keeps telling the boy he is going to school in the fall. This cannot be good if the woman named after a bug thinks it is a good thing.

School is not too bad. But it is a long walk each morning. The worst thing about school is the chores at home when he gets home each day. He thinks often of the pale blue house by the canal and the alfalfa field, and his dime tree, in the magic place called Idaho. Where mother smiled a lot. The older brothers wonder often where mother is and if she ever smiles now. The brothers don't smile much in this place called Kansas.

∞

One windy Kansas day in the spring of 1948, just before the school ended for the year, the letter arrived. Mother was coming to get the boys. The boy wasn't there when the letter arrived, of course, but younger brother was and he ran to the end of the block when he saw older brother poking along on the way home from school. The boy was poking along in an effort, hoping really, to make the chores waiting for him to get done by someone else. They never were but he kept hoping.

He could not believe the news brought to him by his brother. The boy had given up hope of ever being rescued from Kansas, and the house full of women named after bugs and uncles. Most of all father's brother, also called uncle, had a big black belt. The boy dreamed of life somewhere that did not have big black belts.

However, the boy's joy at the news was short lived. As they sauntered along younger brother told him that fathers brother had to say yes or mother couldn't come and rescue them. It seems that fathers brother was something called. "guardian." If he didn't say yes the boys were doomed forever to live in Kansas with the bug women and uncles.

As the boys entered the house all the big people were sitting around the big table where everyone ate and they all seemed to be talking at once, The boys were ignored as they came into the house.

Even baby brother was being ignored and that never happened. One of the bug women always had baby brother in tow.

Finally the noise of the conversation stopped and everyone looked at the two boys standing at the edge of the big room. Fathers brother, the guardian, was not there, he was at work, so grandma spoke to the boys, "well," she said, "it seems your mother has finally remembered she has children. She is coming to get you and your all going to live with her in California."

The two boys stood there in silence for a moment. Then began to jump around shouting together, "Mothers coming, mothers coming." When they finally stopped the older brother thought to himself as he brushed tears from his eyes, "we are wanted, we are not alone, we are rescued". He wondered if mother smiles in this place called California."

CALIFORNIA

There are no memories of the time between the arrival of mother's letter and her arrival in Kansas. But arrive she did and she was smiling.

There is only one vivid memory in the boy's mind of those days between mother's arrival in Kansas and arriving in California. That consists of the train ride from Kansas to California, or at least a portion of that wondrous event. For it is remembered as a most fascinating journey, which the two older brothers never wanted to end.

Baby brother pouted most of the journey because mother had with her a new baby brother who occupied most of her attention. So baby brother no longer occupied the pinnacle of attention he had been used to all of his existence. He was a very unhappy young person. The two older brothers had not yet allowed him into their society, since he had been a major pain in their backsides all of his life up to this point. Therefore, he spent the majority of the journey engulfed in his misery, living with his own company. Yet, it was during this time that he began to be included into the company of his brothers. But, he was still "pruny"

As for the new brother, his name was Dennis, he spent most of the time in his mothers arms, the boy remembers him as being not worthy of much attention. He looked something like a wrinkled pink worm.

While the majority of the journey is a blur of passing landscapes, as the train hurtled through the countryside, with the two older brothers glued to the window, watching America passing rapidly. There was an effort early on by the two older boys, to identify the spot where fathers train wreck had occurred. This was abandoned after they journeyed past Denver. Even at seven and five, they knew they had already gone past the spot where destiny had entered their lives and changed them forever.

The boy remembers vividly one portion of the vista passing so rapidly before him on the other side of the rail coach window. Appearing suddenly one morning and lasting for most of that day. They passed through an area of dessert land covered, as far as the boy's eyes could see, with airplanes of all descriptions, then tanks and big guns, and then trucks and jeeps, Then once again Airplanes and so on. Mother told him they had been brought here after the war was over and moth balled in case they were ever needed again. The boy didn't know what a moth ball was, but it sure took a lot of them to cover all that stuff he had seen out there.

That passage is still clear and vivid a life time later, but the rest to the journey, arrival in California, as well as most of the years in California are lost in the mists of time. The boys memory was becoming much more selective as he grew older. There is a partial memory of the days in California that relates to the previous passage', one of the houses where they boys lived with mother and her new husband and the new pink worm baby brother, had a back yard filled to over flowing with moth balled boats. PT boats, Landing craft with their funny squared nose and other boats of all descriptions. There was a small hole in the fence and the two older boys would crawl through it and play among those boats for hours. One of the strongest memories of this, is the smell of old oil as it dripped from the carcasses of these once magnificent machines. Never did find any moth balls even though the two boys looked diligently for them.

California is a blur of different houses, schools, and childhood events. They are remembered but only as disconnected pictures.

The brothers walking home from a swimming pool through an area of burnt landscape with large tree trunks smoldering as they passed them by. The ground dusty and full of ash, turning their feet black as they walked barefoot through what the boy knows now in his adulthood, must have been a dump of some sort.

Their dog suddenly going missing for what seemed days and days. Only to be found under the house with a whole bunch of puppy's. Mothers new husband taking them all away, never to come home with them. Leaving the boys to wonder where their dog had found all those pups, and where mothers new husband had taken them.

Saturday afternoon at the picture show. The boys could spend all afternoon watching cartoons, serials, and westerns. Gene Autry, Roy Rogers, Hop a Long Cassidy, Lash LaRue. What a wonderful place for the three brothers.

Mother smiled a lot.

The boy passed through the third grade and into the fourth grade, living what now in retrospect, was a nearly normal boyhood, for that time in California, in the years immediately following the war. There are many disconnected pictures, but the indelible memories, the ones that never change are of the last two weeks in California.

It is January 1950.

Mother had gathered the boys together some months past, and told them there was to be another baby. The news was received with mixed results. The two older boys just shrugged their shoulders and hurried outside to continue what ever business they had going at the moment. The younger of the three brothers mopped around for days, for it was clear to him that in this place called California, he had lost his special status as the baby of the family. The newest of the brothers was just too small to even count, as far as the brothers were concerned.

Then Mother was gone.

The grown up woman, who was there to watch over them, told them that morning, their mother had gone to the hospital to get the new baby, and she would be home in a few days.

That night, while the boys were watching wrestling on the new little black and white television. The boy remembers watching "Gorgeous George" getting beat up by some big man wearing a black skin tight mask over his head. He wondered why "Gorgeous George" didn't just pull the mask off so everyone could see the other mans face.

While the brothers were rolling in laughter at the antics of the wrestlers on the television, the woman, who had been there all day, suddenly walked in and turned the television off. As she turned around to face the boys, who were loudly protesting, they grew silent when they saw her face and her tears.

"Boys," She said, "your mother won't be coming home. She died a little while ago as your sister was born."

It was January 8, 1950. (For those who are counting it is just twelve days before the fifth anniversary of fathers death.)

The boys did not say anything, but simply sat there in stunned silence, staring at the blank television set. No one made any effort to comfort the boys and no tears from the boys are remembered. The eldest, as it is remembered thought, "mother will not smile any more." All these years later the boy has amended that thought because he is certain that where ever mother is now she is smiling. He has also come to believe, because it has been demonstrated over and over again, contrary to popular opinion, that there is little if any love in this life.

The boys were not to see their new sister until over twenty years later. They also never saw mother's new husband, the father of their new brother and sister again. A few days after the woman told them mother was dead, the uncle from Kansas and one of the bug women drove into the drive way at the California house. They loaded the three brothers into the car along with their few belongings, and after what is remembered as only a few moments the car whisked them away from California forever and once more back to Kansas.

The boys were silent for most of the trip, speaking only when spoken too, careful not to attract attention. They knew, even the youngest who was never silent knew, they were alone now forever. There was none remaining to rescue them again, only the three remained. They were quiet as they attempted to force their young minds to reason out the finality of the circumstances in which they found themselves.

Childhood had ended for the three brothers. The life of fun and boyhood was now gone. There were no more bikes to ride. No more wrestling on television. No more Cub Scouts and the nice lady who was there to help at each meeting. No more Saturday's at the picture show. No more swimming pool. They wondered if anyone would ever smile at them again. They knew for certain mother never would!

KANSAS ONCE AGAIN

The journey back to Kansas was not a happy trip. Not that it was particularly difficult or that bad things happened. It was just that no one in the car wanted to be there. The three boys certainly would much rather be in California with mother, but knew that was not possible. For sure neither of them wanted to go to Kansas and a life in the house filled with aunts, uncles and a grandma. Any and all memories the three boys had that were associated with Kansas were not pleasant. For the uncle and aunt in the front seat of the car, it was not a trip either had wanted to make. It simply was required. Largely it was an interruption to the routine of their lives, simply to be endured.

So it was not a happy journey.

The boy remembers it as long hours in the car, stopping only to eat and for rest stops as necessary. The only indelible memories are of the petrified forest and the painted desert as they passed through on the highway. They didn't stop!

There is also the unchanging picture of a reddish landscape, with a large tower of rocks where a Navajo Hogan sat beside the road. A few sheep were grassing near the Hogan among the rocky out cropping.

Remembered also is traveling through Dalheart, Texas and across the Texas panhandle into Kansas at night with a bright moon illuminating the interior of the car. Arriving at their destination in that small northwestern Kansas town, the one that had played so frequently in their lives, early in the morning, just after the sun came over the horizon. The house full of aunts and uncles was just beginning to come alive, with all those aunts and uncles and grandma preparing for their day.

The boy has only memories of dullness and drudgery of these days and months. He finished the fourth grade in that small town and in the spring of the year 1950 as school came to an end the boys were told that they were going to Idaho to live with their mothers parents. They would leave the day after school ended for the year.

The news of moving once again was received without comment or emotion, for the three brothers had by this time, learned that they were not wanted. Also, though they did not know how to express it or even what it meant, they knew they were not loved either. The only people in the entire world that had ever loved them, even wanted them, were gone. Never ever to return, and so they turned to each other and the bond was set among the three.

As promised the day after school ended that year, the three brothers were unceremoniously loaded into father's brothers car, with what few belongings they had, and along with fathers brother and one of the bug women, were on the road again headed for Idaho. As they traveled across the countryside of western America, the boy remembered another journey across this same country, on this same highway. A journey toward a magical place called Idaho. However, this time even though they were going to this same Idaho, there was no magic. Magic had disappeared with mother's smile. There was only the journey in the old car with father's brother and one of the bug women.

∞

This was, however, a more relaxed journey than the recent scurry across the country from California to Kansas, They spent the night and breakfasted the next morning in Green River, Wyoming. A memory that for some reason has lasted a life time for the boy, who was now only a month or two from his tenth birthday. He has for some reason, as a result of this always held a soft spot in his heart for Green River, Wyoming.

They once again stopped at "Little America" Wyoming for gas. Little had changed in the five years since his last visit, where mother had also stopped for fuel, and a man called "Soldier" had driven the car on to Idaho so mother could rest.

There was a descent over a canyon rim in to a small Idaho village that sat beside a wide slow moving river. The river wound its way through the village before plunging into rapids as it entered the canyon and continued on its journey west.

This is the boy's first remembered picture of the Snake River, though he is certain in his later years, that he must have encountered this same river during the earlier time in the magic land of Idaho of his past. They spent the night in a roadside motel beside the river in that small Idaho village.

The strangeness of this event which is now so long in the past, is that now in the winter of his years when the boy thinks of the place promised as heaven, the picture which comes to mind is of this small Idaho village with the Snake River meandering slowly through it and the little roadside motel nestled among the weeping willows beside the river.

They arrived at their destination not far from the western edge of Idaho, late in the morning the next day. The last memory the boy has of that journey is of fathers brother and the aunt driving out of the driveway onto the gravel road where mothers parents lived. He stood and watched as the car disappeared down the road. He then turned and joined his brothers as they wrestled and played in the soft blue grass and the white clover of the lawn belonging to their mother's parents.

They somehow knew that now each other was all they had, and that in the morning, life would change forever once again.

IDAHO SUMMER

If you can reach back in your memory to a warm summer evening. When you were full of your childhood and its innocence.

It is early evening, and the sun has began to set. It is that time of day when it is not yet dark, nor is it daylight either.

The warm evening folds itself around you, with a promise of never ending.

It is just such an evening which haunts the boy in the winter of his years.

It is the beginning of summer in the year of 1950 and the place is western Idaho, in the Boise valley region on the north rim of the Snake River.

The place is a small truck farm just east of a town called Nampa. However, it could be any place that draws your memories to where children play in the lush green blue grass on a summer evening.

This was irrigated land and the evening was not a Wednesday, for on that day the lawn was flooded with the life giving water, which made the grass so full and soft and attractive to three young boys. It also could not have been a Sunday evening for play was not allowed on Sunday.

On Sundays after dinner, when the chores were done, and the adults were napping, the three boys would go into the big field next to the house. They would go as far away as they could from the house so their play and laughter would not bother or be stopped by the adults.

There the cotton wood trees at the end of the field. They were big and lush. The cotton woods were wonderful, they had been there many years and had greatly benefited from the outflow of irrigation water from the field. They were huge, providing three growing boys with all sorts of possibilities.

But it is the summer lawn that fills our memory at this moment in time.

The lawn is in front of the home of the three boys maternal grandparents, to which they have been recently transported by their fathers brother.

The boys parents are both dead. They have, in the recent months since their mothers death, been transported from house to house and from one end of the country to the other.

Now the three brothers, nine and a half, seven and a half, and six and a half more or less, roll and tumble in the grass in front of the house. The house which unknown or unnoticed to them is to be home for the next seven years. And which for the rest of their lives, even though as young adults they would scatter far afield never ever to return, would forever be the place they called home.

The gray house, with its lush green lawn, on the small farm in the high mountain desert on the north rim of the Snake River in western Idaho.

Without it ever being spoken, the three brothers knew, all they had remaining in the world was each other. True their basic needs were provided in exchange for labor on the farm. Yet none of that was theirs. None of that belonged to them at all. All they had was each other.

So as often as they could that summer they rolled and tumbled in the grass together.

They were circus acrobats!

They were WWII bomber pilots!

They were Robin Hood and his Merry Band!

They were Cowboys and Indians! Sometimes cowboys and sometimes Indians.

They were Pioneer settlers with their wagon trains and campfires!

They were whatever the imaginations of three fertile young minds could dream up!

That summer they built forts from sod, rocket ships and airplanes from apple boxes and scraps of lumber found lying around the small farm.

They built launchers from old inner tubes tied together and fastened to two small trees planted close together. Great delight was taken by the two oldest in launching the youngest into the air and seeing him momentarily fly across the lawn only to crash with a loud thud into a heap of apple box and scrap lumber. A scrap section of 2X6 does not provide any lift you see.

However, this fact was unknown to the three as they engineered their next craft and prepared to launch their youngest brother into outer space.

For that matter I do not believe they cared that certain engineering skills were lacking. They simply were consumed with their efforts and adventures together. So what if every launch crashed!

They believed that if they just kept trying one day it would work. That it never did was immaterial. When their supplies of apple boxes and scrap lumber were exhausted or they just tired of the game, they simply returned to wrestling and rolling in the grass together.

Eventually, the summer came to a close and school busses appeared to carry them away to different places together, and into the terrors of being the new kids on the bus and in class. There were other summers, six more to be exact. There were more adventures and a fort or two built. Wind cars and boats, even miniature cannons that fired BB's just like the real things.

The three even contrived on one summers day to "safely" hang the neighbor boy, Cory was his name, much to his mothers consternation. They never understood why, but he was never allowed to play with them again. They would just wave across the road to each other.

However, as hard as they would try, there never ever was a summer like that first Idaho summer. As hard as they tried to stop it their world was changing.

The brothers were growing up and becoming individuals with different goals and drives.

However, the three of them never forgot that summer when they were as one. Nor would the bonds that were forged that summer ever be broken. Life brought it changes and challenges, and the bonds were stretched to the limit at times, but never broken.

Yet the oldest is positive that sometimes, in moments of great challenge, even heart ache, each of them in their turn, have paused and in that moment could smell the lush blue green grass and hear the laughter of three small boys as they rolled and wrestled in it, and for just an instant knew they belonged, were wanted and loved.

The two youngest have moved on now, only the oldest remains to tell this tale. Yet when he pauses ever once in a while, he can hear their laughter and smell the grass as they roll around in it and he knows that one day he will join them.

Maybe they will build a rocket ship out of an old apple box. Maybe they will launch it with old inner tubes tied to a couple of old trees and maybe, just maybe this time they will reach the stars.

ADDITIONAL MEMORIES AND THOUGHTS OF IDAHO

Indeed the morning brought major changes for the three boys. The older two entered into a life of what in today's world would result in major legal difficulties for their mothers parents. Theirs was a life of what now could only be described as abuse and indentured servitude.

The youngest of the three escaped most of the servitude since he was considered too small to be of much use, he was just too puny. Also on the one occasion when he was brought to the fields and put to weeding, he had the good sense to cut out every living thing in the row. He had totally destroyed one hundred feet of carrots before the grandmother realized what he was doing and had him banished from the fields forever.

When the older two boys laughed at his antics, as he was escorted from the field by another aunt, they were beaten with the handle of a hoe, until they no longer laughed. Baby brother was not their favorite person after that, and the bond between the older two grew stronger. Each morning as the older two brothers went to the fields at daybreak, the youngest brother watched them go with what can only be described as a self satisfied "shit eating" grin on his face. Intended or not baby brother soon became an enemy of the older two.

The bondage lasted from the early spring of 1950 until the fall of 1956 when the boy ran away, lied about his age and went into the military. This lasted only through basic training, then he was found out and sent back to Idaho. He never, however, went back to live with mothers parents. He flatly refused and was spared going to reform school only when a family, whose son he knew from school, agreed to take him in. He lived with this family only a short time through the winter of 1956-57.

This photo was taken as our protagonist and three other Idaho Air National Guard members were departing Boise, Idaho for basic training. The boy is on the left as you are looking at the picture and his friend Teddy is second from right.

Our young hero as a sixteen and a half year old tough guy while at basic training 1956-57

The other two brothers did not escape, but continued in that world of suffering and abuse until the spring of 1957 when through a series of their eldest brothers misadventures, their Uncle/Guardian learned the truth of their condition and decided he must live up to his responsibilities as their guardian. He appeared quite unannounced one spring morning. Loaded all three boys and their meager belongings into a newer car, along with his wife and their very young son, and it was off to Kansas once more.

∞

There is another memory of those last six years or so in Idaho, it was brought to life recently as the boy was listening to a rendition of "He Ain't Heavy. He's My Brother!", as he and his wife were listening to the Golden Fifties on the car radio as they were traveling somewhere. Memories are strange things, elusive at times, coming and going at will. This song you may know was at the time considered to be the theme song for Boys Town in Omaha, Nebraska. Possibly it still is. I do know there is a statue of a boy carrying another boy on his back with an inscription stating "He ain't heavy he's my brother."

Strange creatures indeed!

Back to the memory.

The boy saw a movie at some point during those years. It stared Micky Rooney and was the story of a boy named "Whitey", who had through several misadventures wound up at Boys Town in Omaha, Nebraska. The boy thinks Spencer Tracy was the priest in the movie, but, that's not relevant to the memory. What is relevant is that as the boy watched the portrayal of life at Boy's Town he found himself engaged completely with the story. He found himself wishing that he and his brothers could live there instead of with his mothers parents. Any life other than the one they had must be better than where they were at that time.

The memories described above of three brothers rolling in the grass are true even though they are idealistic in the telling and they truly are "Semi True Stories". The reality was that the boys were usually bone tired and filthy. The older two came to the yard after a long ten to twelve hour day working in the fields. The youngest joined them out of boredom and loneliness.

They were filthy because they were only allowed one bath a year. This occurred on the night before the first day of school each year. So most of the year they smelled rather loudly. They, however, never noticed because they were used to that condition. All three, when they became old enough for Jr. High, went straight from the bus to the gym and showered each day before classes began. This brought on a major change in their daily lives and relations with others. They then began to accumulate friends, which widened their community beyond just the three brothers.

In September 1957 the oldest of the three brothers joined the United States Air Force. This time all was done correctly and it lasted. The other two, not particularly liked and certainly not loved by their uncle's wife were unceremoniously packed off to an orphanage in an eastern state, which shall remain nameless.

Unfortunately, even though the promise of a bright future for the younger two existed in this new circumstance, it was conditional on their having a successful tenure at this eastern orphanage. However, the die had long since been cast and the mold created, made permanent. The younger two rebelled early and often, any advantage that might have been gained was lost early in their tenure.

The older brother upon being honorably discharged from the United States Air Force sought and gained the guardianship of his two siblings. They lived with him and his family, a wife and small son. While not an entirely peaceful cohabitation, it was finally at last a true home, and they were loved.

The middle brother lived with his brothers and the family until he joined the army in 1962. The baby brother finished high school while living with his eldest brother and remained with the family until he went into the Navy in 1965.

The youngest two have gone on past this life and the oldest wonders sometimes as he remembers the small village beside the Snake River in Idaho and the motel nestled among the weeping willows, if his brothers are there waiting for him. Maybe even Mother and Father. If they are he is certain Mother is smiling.

∞

"Sometimes Life makes us feel alone—On our path through life we are never alone! God is always by our side—"
Rev. Sidney Chambers, Vicar of Grantchester

Brother Bob. On his enlistment into the U.S. Army

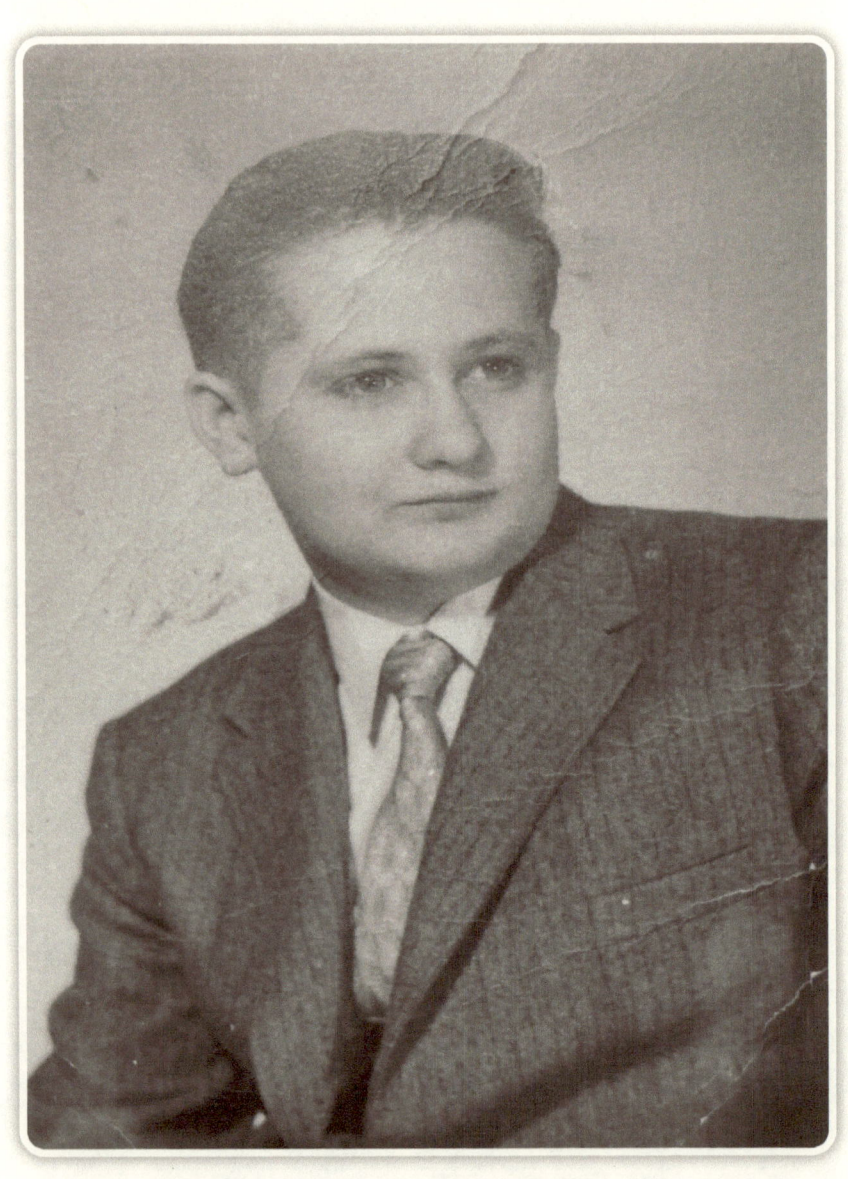

Brother Bill on his graduation from High school

PART I.B

Some Over Laps

SEMI ADULTHOOD

To the boy, it seems that he has always been an adult. Starting maybe from the first return to Kansas after fathers death. Maybe it started at fathers death, but most certainly he was an adult before mothers death. However the realization of this status in his existence didn't occur until years later. This was due largely to the fact that he was to busy putting one foot in front of the other, surviving and helping his brothers to survive also. That seemed to be his only job for more years than he cares to remember.

FIRST JOBS AWAY FROM THE FARM

Some how at the end of the school term in 1955, just prior to the boys fifteenth birthday, he convinced his grandfather to allow him to accept a job as a delivery boy for a Drug Store in town. He was allowed to purchase a bicycle from the Montgomery Ward store as his transportation.

Actually the boy saw the help wanted sign in the window of the store while on lunch break from school. He applied, got the job, and then told his grandparents, knowing due to their new found religious convictions, they would not make him break his word to the store owner. So in effect he "conned" his way off the farm and into his first job, other than forced servitude on the farm. Not sure if he is proud of that now or not, however, it was effective and set into motion many new directions for his feet to travel

It was a marvelous job. Every day, six days a week, he would ride his bike the two miles or so into town and work at the drug store. He washed medicine bottles, stocked shelves, reorganized the basement, but most of all he delivered prescriptions all over town on his bicycle. This got him out of the store and gave him a certain amount of freedom, not to mention money of his own for the first time in his life.

The pay was not much, some where around twenty five dollars a week. The exact amount is not remembered. However, the important part is that this was his money he did not have to give it to his grandparents. They did demand that he give his earnings to them for his support, but he managed to avoid that some how. Exactly how is not remembered.

It was during this summer that the boy mentally, emotionally and socially moved out of his grandparents home, even while still being physically there for some meals and sleeping. There was a restroom with a shower in the drug store where he worked and he took full advantage of it.

He also gathered together a loose collection of friends. None very close, and only one whose name can be remembered all these years later. Yet they all had a good time that summer and their relationship continued into the school year as classes began, even though all were scattered throughout the Nampa school system at various grade levels.

Several nights a week during the summer, the boy would join with a group and go to the drive inn movie located between Nampa and Caldwell, Idaho. The size of the group and its makeup always varied based on several factors.

1. Who had or could get a car for the evening.
2. How large was the car and how large was the trunk.
3. Who had money and who did not.

Once all of these factors were determined, it was decided who was going to ride in the car and pay their way into the theater. Who was to hide in the trunk and who was going to be let out before getting to the front gate, climb the fence and sneak into the theater.

This always varied and the boy had his turn at it all except for driving the car. Often the driver would not have money for the ticket, so everyone who had money would chip in to pay his way. It was a fun filled summer. These evenings extended into the school year until the drive in theater closed for the winter.

The boy rode his Montgomery Ward bicycle everywhere. It was his only transportation. He would meet his friends at a given location, park his bike and join them in the car.

In those days there were City Parks in every town and they were safe places. Most often he would meet his friends at Lake View Park and leave his bike at the park club house.

It was during one of these occasions that he met his first serious girl friend. He was waiting for his friend to pick him up for an evening at the drive in movie. There was a small stream that flowed through the park near the club house. He usually waited on the bank for his friend to arrive. This particular evening there was a group of girls sitting on the bank of the stream chattering away taking little notice of him, being absorbed in their chatter.

He sat down a little distance from them. One of the girls looked at him and smiled. He was instantly smitten. This girl then proceed to move over next to him and introduced herself. No one since Mother had ever shown the slightest interest in him and he was hooked.

Her name was Nelda. To him that was the most beautiful name he had ever heard. She also was very pretty. They chatted until his friend arrived and as luck would have it, that evening there was only the driver and one other boy making a total of three boys going in the car. There were also only three girls, including Nelda. So with his heart in his mouth and for the first time in his life he invited the girls to come with them to the movies. They readily accepted.

There was a free public phone on the back of the park club house, the girls called their parents, got the required permissions and the group was off to the drive in movies. The boy had gotten paid that day so no one had to sneak in that evening.

The details of that evening are long gone from memory, but memories of Nelda have lasted all these years. She was the boy's first love. Their romance by today's standards was very tame. Holding hands, tentative kisses, embraces, but never anything overtly sexual. Both liked the other, respected the other, and genuinely enjoyed each others company. Their romance, if that was what it was, lasted through the boys first entry into the Idaho Air National Guard and his time away at basic training, through his forced return to Kansas and even into his enlistment into the Air Force. During his return to Idaho and while he was waiting for his departure to Lackland Air Force base in Texas, he and Nelda saw each other several times.

After his time at reorientation and his deployment to his first base assignment in Lake Charles, Louisiana. He gathered up the courage to write her a letter asking her to marry him. She refused on the grounds that she was a devout Mormon and would only marry someone of her faith, so that she could marry in the Mormon Temple in Idaho Falls.

It was a crushing blow. The boy could not believe, in all that time together and all of the conversations they had, this subject just never came up. However, he knew her well enough to know she meant what she had said and military life was demanding enough, so he moved on, yet he has never forgot her.

Shortly after meeting Nelda the boy quit his job at the drug store, a big mistake, but not the first or the last. Here the time line of memory gets a little wobbly. Several events seemed to occur almost at the same time. He got a job at the Simplot Packing house. It paid more money, but it was a seasonal job. Lasting only as long as there were crops in the fields needing to be processed for freezing or for market. He remembers first it was onions, then green beans, then lima beans, then sweet peas and so on. He had several different jobs at Simplot always varying with whatever crop was being processed at the time. However, even though whatever he was doing was hard work he didn't mind because he was free. He never returned home after work until late enough to avoid contact with the grandparents, if possible, and he made enough money to feed and entertain himself. By this time he slept on a bed which was either outside next to the house, or in one of the out buildings, so he was not missed. The fact the Simplot job was a seasonal job didn't bother him, since he planned on being gone to the Air Force at the end of the season.

He had saved up some of his money and he bought a motorcycle, for the enormous sum of seventy five dollars. That did not last long. He wrecked it one morning after a night out with one of the wilder boys. They had had to much beer to drink for him to ride the motorcycle home. So he left the bike at his friends house. The next morning, when the dew was heavy on the grass his foot slipped off the peg as he swung his leg over the bike getting on. (The kick starter was broken and the bike had to be pushed in low gear to start it.) He fell to the ground, was drug a few feet before he lost his grip. The bike straightened up and ran on its own about a hundred feet, at full throttle, into the side of a house. The front fork was twisted beyond repair. That was the end of the first motorcycle. The boy sold it to another friend for parts for fifty dollars.

A few evenings later, on a Saturday night, the boy was in the living room of his grandparents house waiting for his friends to pick him up. His Grandfather asked him what he was doing. The boy responded telling him that some of the guys were coming by and they were all going to the drive in.

Grandfather informed the boy in no uncertain terms, he was going nowhere! It was Saturday night and he had to go to church in the morning.

That was the final straw. The boy in no uncertain terms, in words of no more than one syllable, many starting with the letter "F", told his mothers father just what he thought of his church and where exactly he could put it. He got up and walked out of the house. His friends arrived moments later, he got in the car telling them to "Get the hell out of here fast." Which they did, as grandfather chased them down the road waving his arms, and the boy responded with an appropriate gesture, using his hand and a certain digit.

It was three weeks before he returned, escorted by two sheriffs deputies.

The boy spent those weeks moving from one friends house to another and at times sleeping rough in the park, but he was determined he was never returning to that house of horror again.

However, It seems the grandfather was not willing to lose slave labor that easily, so he called the law when the boy did not return. The only thing he could think of to tell the sheriff was that the boy had run way on a motorcycle, the boy had bought, but he did not have a drivers license. That part was true, but the boy did not own the bike any longer, and he did not run away on it.

Anyway three weeks later while passing through down town in a car with a couple of friends, he was spotted, arrested, put in jail for the night, and then brought back to his mothers parents farm in handcuffs. The cuffs were used because the deputy's knew that given the slightest chance, the boy was gone again.

His arrival at the farm was met with great hilarity by his brothers, which was immediately corrected with beatings around their heads with a broom, wheeled by grandmother. Grandfather greeted the deputies with a most devilish self-satisfied grin.

The boy had been told by the deputies that if he ran away again he would be in big trouble, they repeated this again, removed the cuffs and departed.

The next few days were pure hell, but the boy had a plan.

The boy had an acquaintance from school. The boy knew him as "Teddy". Teddy had a last name, but, it is not important for this telling.

Teddy had quit school. He simply did not return at the beginning of the school term in 1956. The boy ran into him by accident one evening just before the sheriffs deputies found him.

Teddy had gotten a job with the Union Pacific railroad working in the rail yard in Nampa as a switch-man trainee. Teddy had also joined the Idaho Air National Guard. He had suggested to the boy that he should join the guard also. So this was the plan.

The boy would join the Idaho Air National Guard and request basic training as soon as the first class opened. This would take him to San Antonio, Texas for three months. Then as the training time came to an end, he would request transfer to full time active duty, and would then be assigned to a base somewhere far from the Idaho farm. He would be gone for years and planned to never return.

One big problem. The boy was not old enough to join anything but the Boy Scouts. So how could this plan be activated?

The boy with the help of his friend Teddy devised a plan which required him to lay low until the dust settled and his moves would not be suspicious, until he was just simply gone again. This he did and one day he approached his grandmother, convinced her to sign a paper which stated she was his legal guardian, some what true, and that he was over seventeen years of age. She was not aware of that part. So far so good. Now he just had to wait and attend guard meetings until an opening came available to go off to basic training.

How he managed all this he cannot remember but he did. Then at the Guard meeting in August, he was given orders to report one morning in early September to travel to basic training. His friend Teddy was also going at the same time. So one morning in early September 1956 the boy met his friend Teddy at the side of the road not far from the farm and he was gone. This time he hoped for good..

In fairness it should be said that from the time the boy was approaching fifteen until his ultimate departure, he gave his mothers parents as much of a hard time as he could, but in fairness it should also be said that they deserved all he gave them and more.

Upon arrival at Lackland Air force Base his friend Teddy was assigned to a different training group called a Flight", and due to the events which followed he never saw Teddy again.

Basic training was much as one might expect, a radical learning curve. However, the plan was working. A week or so before training ended the boy approached his Drill Instructor as planned and made his request to transfer into the active U. S. Air Force. This was received with the proper amount of berating by the Drill Sargent, but none the less submitted up the chain of command.

A few days later, just a few days before time to be shipped back home and the Idaho Air National Guard, the boy was summoned to the Commanders Office. He spiffed up his uniform and appearance, to the height of military spit and polish, and presented himself at the appointed time to the Duty Officer and the First Sargent. Both were very reserved in their reception and this cooled the boys expectations of being transferred to active duty. His hopes were not killed, however, because why else would he be summoned into the presence of the squadron commander.

Moments later he was escorted into the commanders office. He saluted, and was told to stand at ease. He stood there with the commander looking at him in a most agitated manner. As best memory serves the one sided conversation went something like this.

" Well Airman I see you have requested active service rather than return home".

"Yes Sir".

"Well Airman, I would be happy to sign off on your request as soon as you are of legal age to be accepted into any active military service"!

The boy stood there in total shock. How had they found out?

The Commander continued, "you did quite well and no one should have ever known. However, do you remember the photographs you were required to have made"?

"Yes Sir".

"Well Airman, those were sent to your local newspaper as a matter of recruiting policy, and since it seems you had disappeared without a trace, your relatives were on the alert. An uncle of yours saw your picture, told your grandparents and now here you are. Since you are here as Nation Guard it's up to them to deal with you. For our part you will complete your training as scheduled, and be sent back to Idaho as scheduled at the end of the week. Dismissed".

The boy was escorted back to the barracks in utter disillusion. The only bright spot was that all of his superiors stated they thought he would make a good Airman, when he grew up.

A few days later the boy was standing in front of the commander of the Idaho Air National Guard in Boise Idaho. He doesn't remember that conversation, but he found himself very quickly standing on the street with his discharge papers in his hands. Fortunately, because of his good record during basic, it was an Honorable discharge rather than something more harsh.

He was met on that street by another Sheriffs deputy, who escorted him back to Nampa, and his mothers parents house. But this time he flatly refused to get out of the car, telling the deputy to take him straight to jail. Stating, "I would rather be in prison, than spend one minute in that house"!

Again, fortunately for him, this deputy was an understanding man and instead took him to the uncle who lived in Nampa. The one that had seen his picture in the paper and caused the collapse of the plan. He was a well known business person in town, and well liked. This uncle allowed him to make a couple of phone calls. Arranging for a place to live with a family, who's son had been friends with the boy before he quit school.

∞

Shortly after these events had settled down the Boy needed to get a drives license. The family he lived with could not sign for him as they were not court appointed and had no legal status where he was concerned. Even though they would have done so if they could have done it without getting into legal trouble, a couple of mother's brothers were continually making threats.

So, even though his instincts told him not to do it, the Boy wrote to Uncle Bo, asking him to sign the permission slip enclosed in the letter. Of course he also had to tell Uncle Bo to mail the slip back to the address where he was currently living. Otherwise he would never receive it for mothers parents would never admit they had received it. So the game was afoot as Sherlock is often quoted as saying.

The boy never received a reply from Uncle Bo. Instead one morning early as the boy and the family he was residing with were eating breakfast, there was a knock on the door. When the knock was answered, there stood Uncle Bo on the front stoop, with his wife Francis in the car with the motor running.

In due course the whole story was told, the Boy's meager belongings packed, goodbyes said, a tear or two shed and they were off to mother's parents house to rescue brothers Bob and Bill.

This also was accomplished in rather quick fashion, however, with a great deal of very loud protest from mother's relations. Yet before the sun set on that day the three brothers, The Boy's", were well east of Nampa Idaho and on their way to Kansas once more. However this time would be the last time.

Except for the visit with his uncle, to rescue his brothers in the early spring of 1957, and one five minute visit, at the request of his uncle in Nampa, two days before entering the Air Force in September 1957 the boy never ever set foot in that house again. He turned his back on Idaho in 1957 returning only in 1982, as required by his employment at the time.

This is the "Boys" and Uncle Bo's family shortly after arriving in Goodland Kansas for the last time and prior to our protagonist's entry into the Air Force. Summer 1957. Foreground left to right, brother Bob and brother Bill. Background left to right The Boy, Grandma Linnell (Margret O'Brian Linnell) Mark, (uncle Bo's son) Francis(uncle Bo's wife) and Uncle Bo.

KANSAS FOR THE LAST TIME

During the spring and summer of 1957 the boy lived with his brothers and fathers brother, "Uncle BO", and his family in Goodland, Kansas. That is part of the time. Uncle BO found him a job driving a tractor on a farm just outside of town. He also helped him get his drivers license and purchased his first car. The car was a black 1947 Chevy four door sedan. Not the coolest style, but it was his.

This was a very busy time and is filled with lots of partial memories.

The Bowling Alley, girls, the smell of fresh turned earth as the tractor moved across the field, girls. Being caught in a sudden thunder shower without time to get to the end of the field. The tractor getting stuck. Walking in the mud to the end of the field to the car, while the farmer on the other side of the road continued on with the dust flying with never a drop of rain, girls.

The local A&W, cold root Beer, a pork tender sandwich ordered as; "Pork on two" to split with his buddy "Woody", girls.

The boy was a fresh face in town and after work either at the movies, the bowling alley or the A&W there were always plenty of girls.

His buddy "Woody" worked on a farm north and east of the little town Brewster, Kansas. Goodland was the closest town of any size so that is where he came for entertainment. The boy met "Woody" one Saturday evening after the brothers returned to Kansas. They hit it off pretty much instantaneously and became fast friends. During those few months of the spring and summer of 1957 they were pretty much inseparable. Where you found one you found the other.

Eventually, Woody got the boy work on the same farm where he worked. Those were good days and the best of times. Long days, hard work, good companionship, equally long hours at play on their time off. Driving to Goodland, movies, etc, and girls, girls.

Woody was equally as popular as the boy. It seemed there was always a line of girls waiting for the two to arrive in Goodland on Friday night. They stayed at Uncle BO'S house for the weekend. The boy had his room in the big cool basement. There were a couple of comfy beds, a bath with a shower, and a private entrance. Just what two guys on the prowl needed.

They would arrive at Uncle BO's on Friday evening, just long enough to drop off their things, say hello, and head to the A&W for "Pork on Two", and to view the "girl" menu for the weekend. The only draw back to the girl menu was that the boy had to check with his uncle's wife before dating any of the girls. It seems he was "cousin" to a large portion of them.

They would depart on Sunday afternoon or early evening so they could get back to the farm in Brewster in time to get some rest before the work week started again. While they were in Goodland they always found time to help the two younger brothers with their paper routes, on Saturday and Sunday morning. Loading the car up with papers and all four covering the town with the Rocky Mountain News in record time.

Woody was a year or two older than the boy and was part of the Kansas National Guard. Because he was a farm worker he was exempt from Guard Meetings every month during the summer season and harvest. However, in late August of that year he had to attend the two week annual training session. The boy had made it known to Woody that at the end of harvest he intended to return to Idaho and enlist in the Air Force. He didn't need to return to Idaho to do that, but he had made a promise to a recruiting Sargent, and he felt duty bound to honor the promise.

So, on a hot clear morning at the beginning of the third week of August 1957, the two friends said goodbye as Woody headed off for the two weeks of Guard camp. The boy never again saw his friend, the only true friend he had ever had. Woody was killed a few years later in Vietnam while the boy was in Thule Greenland. How Woody managed to get to Vietnam he never found out but he was there never the less at the very beginning, at a time when officially we didn't even have troops in that country, only "advisors". What a screwed up world we live in.

The boy stayed behind working on the farm for another week. He had given his notice and at the end of the week he loaded his belongings into his 1947 Chevy and headed to Goodland. A few days later he climbed into a Greyhound bus on main street in Goodland, Kansas and headed once more to the fabled land of Idaho.

That was the end of one of the brightest periods of the boy's life. There were to be more, but this time has always been the bench mark against which all else was measured.

PART II

Adulthood

(at least that's what it's called)

MILITARY SERVICE AND GIRLS

As stated earlier adulthood was thrust upon the three brothers at a very early age, even it could be said in the case of the younger brother, before he had ever been born. Certainly for all three before childhood had even begun properly. Certainly for the oldest, it began in earnest upon his entrance into the US Air Force. It was at this juncture in his life that he became truly and totally responsible for himself with no one controlling his life and the decisions he made. Good bad or indifferent, and there have been many of both, he alone and no one else was involved. There were no Uncles or bug women telling him what to do. No grandparents or Guardians, just himself. The boy can remember how wonderful that felt. That feeling and condition of being, had been sought by the boy for most of his life. He embraced it with open arms and an excitement that only the extreme fallacy of youthful arrogance can bring.

A few things about military service and girls

1. The boy is from a generation of whom military service was a given. Upon completion of high school, it was expected that one either went to collage or entered the military. If you went to collage it was expected that you joined the service after collage. That was simply the way of life for the boys generation.

    If you quit school you entered the military as soon as possible. No question.

2. As long as the boy could remember he had decided, the only route of escape from the life in the fields and the tyranny

of his mothers parents, was military service. Because of this belief he counted the days and worked out many scenarios for how he could do this as soon as he could.

3. Have I mentioned Girls? There are more than a few things about girls. Most of them are still a closely guarded secret after all these years. Who guards the secret is also a secret. So most of the mystery about girls is still a mystery to the boy even now in the winter of his years.

    Largely because of the living conditions under which he grew up the boy never had a "girl friend", until he met Nelda. So that relationship, though remembered only in the most loving way possible, was never meant to be what could be described as normal. Because of the circumstances of his formative years the boy always had the need for belonging and to be loved. This colored every "adult" relationship throughout his life. However, because of the gross abnormality of those years compared to others, he never really knew how to belong, or to be loved or give love. All that he knew came from books or the movies, not the best of models for relationships.

4. Somehow largely because of the generational thing, the boy grew up with the idea the if you had sex with a girl, you got married. Any relationship that would lead to or resulted in sex, had to be culminated in marriage. So for many years the boy lived life on a tight rope. Balancing between the worlds of a youthful sex drive and the need to marry. Frustrating to say the least. While he knew that not everyone lived this way, he believed it to be the only way. So casual dating was simply not in the picture, let alone casual sex. God forbid!

    Largely because of this, and the fact that he is not the easiest person to live with, there have been several wives and many almost wives over the years.

SEPTEMBER 3, 1957 THE US AIR FORCE FOR REAL!

The boy returned to Idaho. His first stop was the recruiter in Boise. Then he spent a few days visiting friends, mostly Nelda.

On the morning of September 3,1957 the boy along with several others boarded a Union Pacific Passenger train at the station in Boise and headed south and the rest of the story. One foot in front of the other.

While the boy had earned his own way for some years, entry in to the Air Force, marked by getting onto that train, was the beginning of true adulthood. Responsibility! From that point on there was no fall back plan. Wherever life brought. Wherever it led, he and he alone was responsible. Success or failure, it was his alone.

He arrived at Lackland Air Force Base, San Antonio, Texas a couple of days later, and was assigned to a retraining squadron, since he had already completed basic training once. What he had not anticipated was that he was the youngest and least experienced in the group. All the rest of those in the barracks were several years older. All retreads from service of at least one hitch, and a few with two or three hitches. The result was that there were few if any common experiences, and once again he was alone in the crowd. However, he survived the 45 days or so he was there while officialdom determined where he was to fit in.

Eventually, one morning after returning from "chow", as he checked the bulletin board there was his name next to his assignment and date of departure.

A/3 Kenneth D. Linnell
Chanualt Air Force Base, Lake Charles, Louisiana
Reporting date 11/15/1957
Assignment Base Motor pool
MOS 60350 Veh. Oper.

A Few days later he had his orders and pay records as well as two months pay, ($150.00), in his hot little fist. Along with instruction from a very scary female Sargent at the pay office, " to guard those

F-----g records with your life". This he did because she also told him, there was an even scarier pay officer at Lake Charles, waiting for those records.

So there he was a full fledged, newly minted Airman Third Class, standing at the Gates to Lackland Air Force Base with a brand new stripe on each arm of his stiffly starched and creased class "A" uniform, with ten days to kill before he had to report to his permanent duty station.

So what would you do?

What he did was get on a bus and go to Dallas/ Ft. Worth and the Texas State Fair.

He had been on the grounds only about an hour when he walked over to the base of "Big Tex" and there she was sitting beside the left foot, looking like a million dollars, with a smile that was all his. He doesn't remember her name, but she worked as an operator for "Ma Bell", why he remembers that and not her name, who knows. A week later he crawled onto a south bound bus totally wrung out, but with a big smile, and headed for Lake Charles, LA and some much need rest.

CHENNAULT AIR FORCE BASE, LAKE CHARLES, LA

As he remembers he arrived in Lake Charles, LA late in the evening. It was a week day, but he can't remember exactly which one.

As he got off the bus and entered the station two things caught his attention. Two water fountains one marked "Whites Only" and the other marked "Colored Only". Also there were four rest rooms all marked in the same way. This was his first clash with southern race segregation.

He went into the small cafe and asked the waitress how to get to the base. She told him to catch the city bus just out side the front door of the station, and one would be by in about thirty minutes.

He thanked her and ordered a cup of coffee. She asked if he wanted regular or black. He had been drinking black coffee since he was 10 years old, and still does, so he told her black. She smiled and poured his coffee. He went over to a table by the window to watch for the bus. He raised the coffee to his lips and blew on it to cool it a little and took a good sip, swallowed. He thought he had been poisoned. He involuntarily spewed what remained in his mouth all over the table, as the waitress approached with a towel to wipe up the mess, laughing with every step. His first introduction to Cajun dark roast coffee. The bus arrived, he left the remains of the coffee and boarded the bus for the base.

He arrived at the main gate about 30 minutes later was checked in with military precision and installed in the transit barracks for the night.

Early the next morning, everything happens early in the morning in the military, he reported to the indeed scary payroll Sargent, with the ever closely guarded pay records. He was congratulated in a rather cool manner, for having preserved and presenting his records intact. He was then informed he would have to wait until the records were processed for his pay. He was told to report back to the payroll office after he had completed processing onto the base, in about three days. In the mean time he was given directions to the transit mess hall for his meals and to his assigned duty squadron headquarters.

All of this was received in a slight daze as the payroll Sargent was very scary indeed. As an aside during his entire career in the military he never met a payroll officer who wasn't scary as H—l.

༄

A few days later he was waiting to see the First Sargent in the very small vestibule of the Base Motor Pool. As he waited he listened in awe to a smallish round black man, who was to become a good friend and mentor, even though the acquaintance lasted only a few months, as he answered the phone. This is what he heard every time this man answered the phone.

> *"Good Morning Sir! You have reached the base motor pool dispatch service, Staff Sargent Aloyious T. Clay speaking. We have everything to meet your need. We got, 2 buys, 4 buys, 6 buys, and 8 buys. We even got them big mother f----rs that split in the middle and go choo-choo, How can I help you today"?*

The boy couldn't believe what he was hearing and barely controlled his laughter.

As it turned out some weeks later Staff Sargent Clay was teaching the boy to drive a large wrecker, one used to recover aircraft after a crash. He then learned that Sargent Clay had been a driver in the famous "Red Ball Express" during WWII and he was retiring in six months and to coin a phrase, "he just didn' t give a damn."

Eventually the boy waiting to see the First Sargent, became important enough to be called into the presence. The royal title is used here because the "First Shirt" as he was called out of his hearing, was indeed royalty in the chain of command. Nothing happened without his involvement. Even the Squadron commander, a non nondescript first lieutenant, did nothing without consulting the "First Shirt".

He was promptly informed the there was no room in the squadron for him at that time, so he was being reassigned temporarily to the Air Police squadron, and given his papers and directions to the Air Police duty office.

So there he was once more standing on the street with orders in his hand, wondering just what the hell he had gotten himself into. He had been in Lake Charles only a few days during which he had, nearly been poisoned by the coffee, screamed at by a very scary payroll Sargent, he was broke because he had spent most all of his pay in Dallas on a very lovely women, and he still hadn't been paid. He had reported in to his duty assignment, waited for over an hour and then shown the door because, "there was no room for him." The only thing he had learned, which he would never forget, about the base motor pool, was how to answer the phone from Staff Sargent Aloyious T. Clay,

> *"Good Morning Sir! You have reached the base motor pool dispatch service, (insert name here). We have every thing to meet your need. We got, 2 buys, 4 buys, 6 buys, and 8 buys. We even got them big mother f----rs that split in the middle and go choo-choo, How can I help you today"?*

AIR POLICE

He arrived at the Air Police duty office a short time later, it was just a short walk, you walked everywhere. There was a shuttle bus service, however it ran indifferently, so you never knew when it would come around. Therefore the quickest and usually the shortest route was to just walk.

At the Air Police duty office he was confronted by another First Sargent, and for the first time welcomed to the squadron, the base and even the Air Force. What a difference a smiling face and a hand shake can make.

He was told he was to be assigned to Flight Line Security and Flight Number three. (at that time every "squad" was called a flight in the Air Force.) They were currently on their days off as they worked a three day rotation and would return to duty in two days. In the meantime he was given his barracks assignment, a note to the supply clerk for his bedding and other duty related gear, and most important of all his mess hall pass. He was told to report to the duty Office at 08:00 in the morning for orientation and to begin OJT (on the job training) for Flight Line Security.

He thanked the First Shirt and walked over to the supply clerks office where he was issued his bedding, a couple of Air Police arm Bands, a holster complete with a web belt, a .45 caliber automatic hand gun and an M1 Carbine rifle. He was loaded for bear. No ammunition however.

He walked out of the Duty Office, arms full and noticed over the pile of bedding, that the Payroll office was just across the street. He found the barracks, deposited his new belongings in his new room, and walked across the street to see if the Scary Sargent would give him his pay. He did! A short time later he was once again standing on the street considering what to do next. This did not take long for it was now noon time and his stomach was telling him it was time to find the Mess Hall, which he did.

⌘

Chennault Air Force Base in 1957 was a bomber base and therefore Strategic Air Command. When the boy assumed his duties in flight line security, the parking pads (flight line) next to the runway were filled to over flowing with huge air planes. There were a few B-36's which were gigantic, but these were quickly being replaced with sleek fighter like B-47's.

His job, in what ever kind of weather, was to guard four of these aircraft from whomever or whatever. He walked around his four aircraft on an ever varying path for twelve hours. He worked three days on and two days off. The shifts during those three days were broken up by rest breaks every four hours with a mess (meal) break in the middle. In other words he would walk his beat for three hours have a one hour rest break, back on the beat for three hours another rest break etc.

SAC took its security seriously in those days, he was always armed with a loaded hand gun and an M1 carbine, with orders to shot if necessary. The ammunition was checked in and out at the beginning of each duty session.

It was a good life. It was also a good place to learn about the world into which he now found himself. The work wasn't hard, even though it could be intense at times, such as when an alert was called and all the aircraft had to be armed and gotten airborne asap.

It was hard to keep up in those conditions, because there were all sorts of people around doing various things and they all had to be challenged and deemed to be in their appropriate place for the moment. But the excitement made up for the extra work.

There is nothing like standing at the edge of the runway watching as the pilot turns a large bomber onto the runway and just as quickly pushes it to full throttle, racing toward you with all engines roaring, shaking the ground beneath your feet. Then just before this roaring monster reaches the half way point, just as the wings begin to lift, the pilot flips a switch and the rocket bottles(JATO) mounted to the belly of the air craft come to life with a thunderous roar. Unbelievably, this roaring, graceful monster, leaps almost vertically from the runway climbing into the sky on a column of dense smoke, so fast the huge plane was gone covering you in rocket and jet fuel smoke and fumes, before you could regain the breath that was stolen as it passed.

A sight and a memory made indelible in the mind of the boy.

The boy worked Flight Line Security for ninety days and at the end he didn't want to leave, but despite his desires, he was given back to the motor pool a few weeks before Staff Sargent Clay retired. He was placed at Sargent Clay's disposal for training and in those few remaining weeks Staff Sargent Clay, with a tough hand and a cloud of profanities, did his best to make a vehicle operator of the boy.

Chennault Air Force Base and Lake Charles, LA was the only state side duty station the boy had while in the Air Force, since SAC did not move it's people around much, at least in the States.

However, the boy became a world traveler while stationed at Lake Charles, because there was this thing called "TDY", short for temporary duty assignment and the "Strike Force". Remember these were the days of the "Cold War".

Shortly after returning to the motor pool he was assigned to a "Strike Force". This mostly meant that every time an alert, which was at least twice a month, was called he had to report to the flight line with his bags packed. Usually, he along with many others, would load onto the KC 97 tankers, bag and baggage, headed to "Curt LeMay and God only knew" where, General Curtis Lemay was commander of SAC in those days.

Some of the time they would just fly a pattern out over the Gulf of Mexico, always refueling a few B-47's before landing and returning to normal. However, there were frequent occasions when something going on during those "Cold War" days would get the leaders excited and he would wind up in strange and wonderful places. Most often because of the target assignment to Second Air Force and Chennault's two B47 wings in particular. the boy would wind up for a few days in Goose Bay Labrador or Gander Newfoundland. Occasionally he would find himself in places like, The Azores, Spain, England, even Thule Greenland once. There never was a chance for site seeing, only what could be seen from the aircraft windows during take off and landing. During these deployments you were either working or secured in the barracks. Once he landed in Goose Bay and was transported in blacked out vehicles along with two hundred other men to an underground barracks and mess hall were they stayed for four days waiting further orders.

I think that was one of the times Nikita was pounding the lectern at the UN, with his shoe, telling us he was going to bury us.

Anyway, the boy would be gone for a few days or weeks at a time, then be back as if nothing had happened. It certainly kept life interesting.

There were also some ninety day TDY assignments as well, several to Goose Bay, Labrador and one to Clinton-Sherman Air Force Base located between Clinton and Elk City Oklahoma. That was an assignment that changed the boys life forever.

However, life in the Air force, and particularly in Lake Charles, was not all work and no play.

Lake Charles in the winter of 1957-58 being located as it is in the westernmost Parish in Louisiana was like any good respecting town south of what now is I-10, but in those days was any thing in and around U.S. Highway 90. That is, it is Cajun country, and combined with the free rolling Cajun culture and the Louisiana motto of "

Laisse Les Bons Temps Rouler", or "Let the good times roll/ make merry" there were numerous dance halls, bars, and lounges where a young man could spend his off duty time and money. A great place for a young man learning to have a good time. And did I mention girls?

The boy quickly developed his list of favorite haunts, but his favorite was a crowded little Cajun flavored lounge just around the corner form the Greyhound Bus station, affectionately known as the "Scrounge Lounge". Not the real name, but the one assigned by all the locals and servicemen who were the patrons. Here the desired adult beverages flowed freely, while a four piece group played a mixture of rock and roll, jazz, Zydeco, and anything else they thought would fit in. This music was also given an affectionate name by everyone, "Coon A-s Stomp". If you didn't have a good time at the "Scrounge Lounge" you were dead!

And did I mention Girls?

Cajun women are notorious for their good looks and their love of having a good time. "Laisse Les Bon Temps Rouler."

It was there at the Scrounge Lounge one evening in early 1958 that the boy met "Emily" and the good times rolled for a while. Emily was to become official wife number one. It didn't last long however, a few weeks later the boy found himself moving back into the barracks, asking himself what the hell had happened.

That was not a question for long. It was answered one morning bright and early when the "First Shirt" called the boy into the squadron office and loudly wanted to know why the Squadron Commander was getting calls from, "Your Wife", demanding to know when her allotment would arrive?

As meek and sincerely as possible he explained the situation to the First Shirt and received a response something like this. "Well another one falls to the Scrounge Lounge and the Cajun women. That damn place should be put off limits! (The fact that it wasn't was due to it being owned by the long time incumbent mayor). You need to know, that until you can get a divorce, and that will take a hell of a long time in this state, you will have to support her. She will get half your pay, plus an additional amount for "off base" housing etc. So Airmen you may not be drunk or disgusted, but you are officially screwed and broke. I would also advise you to stay clear of the Scrounge Lounge."

This last part was not hard to do, for very shortly the boy found out that half of seventy five dollars per month didn't even stretch to a months worth of cigarettes, and they were only ten cents a pack at the PX, let alone nights at the Scrounge Lounge.

As always the First Shirt was right and a year later the boy finally got the divorce and the allotment stopped, but he had to file in, and go to Kansas to get it, and tell a fib or two under oath, but he got it.

By now he had gotten a promotion and was an Airman Second Class, that's two stripes and One Hundred ten dollars a month. In the money again and store bought cigarettes.

Have I mentioned girls?

About this time the opportunity came along to go TDY for ninety days to a new base SAC was opening in western Oklahoma. It was a new B-52 wing and volunteers were needed to get it up and running until permanent duty personnel could be gathered together, and it paid extra per-diem also. Sounded like a plan to the boy, who thought getting out of town and away from the Cajun temptations was a good idea. So he stepped right up and volunteered, (something you never ever do in the military), and 36 hours later he was on a Grey Hound Bus headed to Clinton, Oklahoma.

Wherever the hell that was!

The route took him through most of east and central Texas. There was a long layover in Dallas with a young woman, also a passenger on the bus, who for some reason thought him to be neater than sliced bread. So, once again the boy arrived at his destination broke, but not disgusted or drunk. However, in need of some rest.

It turns out that the new base was some distance from Clinton, Oklahoma at a place called Foss. So the boy called the number listed by the pay phone in the Greyhound Bus Station lobby for "Base Transportation", and went into the cafe for some coffee, while he waited for someone to come pick him up.

Have I ever mentioned girls?

There she was! The waitress working diligently behind the counter. She was tall, slightly freckled with reddish blond hair and a figure that filled out her uniform in a way that made the boys eyes water. He ordered coffee and pie and did everything he could do to get her attention, however she was to busy or just not interested. He made a vow, that if he ever got back to this town, he was going to get this girl to go out with him. Somehow.

His ride came and a few hours later he was duly installed in the Transportation Squadron Barracks on Clinton-Sherman Air Force Base, Foss Oklahoma.

It was two or three weeks before he got any time off and since he didn't have his own transportation he had to hitch hike the 15 or so miles into town. However, in due course he did just that and went straight to the Bus Station Cafe. She was not there. So he walked around town went to a movie and back to the Bus Station a couple of times. Since he didn't know her name he couldn't leave a message so he just kept going back.

It was his third trip to town and about half way through his 90 days when he arrived at the bus station and there she was. He quickly sat down at the counter and ordered coffee and pie, but this time he was determined to get her attention.

He did and discovered her name was Lucy. She was not busy that afternoon, so she seemed eager to talk to him. He learned that her middle name was Lucille. Mildred was her first name, but she went by Lucy because she didn't like Mildred. He found out that her shift ended at 6 pm and he got up the courage to ask her if she would go to the movies with him. She said she would, but she had to go home and change first, as well as he would have to meet her father, before she could go out with him. He explained he didn't have a car so they would have to walk, that was OK with her so the date was made.

A short time later he found himself in the living room of her home. Her father and mother had been introduced as well as her siblings. He'd met the whole family. Now he was waiting for her to get ready. Her father who was an officer on the Clinton Police Force was stretched out on the sofa on the other side of the room. He was just laying there staring at him, not saying a word. He was a big man, wearing a gun, the message was loud and clear.

Fortunately, Lucy, finally made her appearance and they hurried out the door. After that introduction the boy never understood why he was still there, but he was and even though he returned to Lake Charles at the end of his temporary assignment, the romance continued. He and Lucy were married June 10,1959, at the First Baptist Church, in Clinton Oklahoma, shortly after the end of her Junior year in high school,

Two days later he was back on duty in Lake Charles, LA standing in front of the First Shirt attempting to explain why he was once again married, without first asking permission of the U. S. Air Force.

To say that particular interview did not go well is an understatement. He was saved only by the First Shirt being impressed with the particular circumstances and promises made to Lucy's mother in order to get her permission for the wedding. Actually he began to laugh half way through the explanation eventually giving up and telling the boy to get the hell out of his sight. Which he did quickly.

Lucy was very adept at getting her way with her parents. Once she had decided on a particular thing they didn't stand a chance. So, she had promised her mother, if she were allowed to marry our protagonist, she would remain at home until she had finished high school and the boy's enlistment was up. Her mother bought into that. (poor deluded woman). She also promised that she would not get pregnant until after she finished school, (even more delusional in "pre-pill" days).

Our boy truly loved his "Lucy", more truthfully he was totally enthralled with her, while not a beauty queen, she was as lovely as any 16 year old in the world, and he was completely wrapped around her little finger. He would agree to anything. So there he was back in Lake Charles just short of his 19th birthday, married, divorced, and married again.

Have I ever mentioned girls?

It soon became apparent that Lucy had no concept of what life in the military was like and its restrictions. If the boy, her husband as she frequently pointed out, was off duty she wanted him to be with her. Not a problem except the Clinton, Oklahoma is some 630 miles distant and there was no way that was going to happen. In early August of that year the boy was given a 90 day TDY assignment to Goose Bay, Labrador, thus solving that problem for at least three months.

It was an uneventful three months marked only by a huge forest fire west of the base which caught the tundra on fire. This burned and smoldered for weeks but eventually it began to rain and then snow, which put it out and the 12 hour shifts ended.

Lucy also had made some connections at Clinton-Sherman Air force base. She also had discovered the WATTS telephone service. This was a system by which the command centers could call any military base in the world. It was a 24/7 service and was used by the servicemen to call home occasionally. Of course military traffic took priority, but it was a good way to stay in touch with home when you were far away.

It will only be said here that Lucy misused this immensely, once she discovered how to use the system. Even to the point that one of the operators told the boy to calm that woman down or he would be subject to an Article 15 (an in squadron punishment). He told her to cool it, but to no effect. No one in the Air Force was going to tell her what to do.

At the end of his 90 day assignment he, along with others, loaded onto a KC-97 and took off for Lake Charles, LA and Chennault Air Force Base once more. In due course they landed and taxied through the familiar B-47's to the pad in front of the base flight center. The boy grabbed his gear and walked to the Fight Ops. Center to get a ride to his squadron office, to report in.

There before him was Lucy. She ran and embraced him as if he had just returned from the wars. All he could do was ask himself, "How the hell did she get here?"

That question never was completely answered, but there she was. So they caught a ride and went to the Squadron office, reported in, caught another ride to the front gate, then the bus to her motel, just outside the base.

The next several months were consumed with balancing the Air Force and married life in Lake Charles, LA. This was mostly taken up in pretending that whatever domestic endeavor was entered into was not subject to destruction at any moment by the Air Force. Lucy was determined to counter act anything the Air Force attempted to do.

It was during this time that the boy first realized there was another side to his lovey wife named Mildred. Mildred's motto was "Who the Hell do you think you are to tell me what to do?" However, during this time Mildred did not appear often, so the boy and his Lucy thoroughly enjoyed each other and their life in Lake Charles.

However, eventually the Air Force intervened and orders came in November requiring the boy to report to Thule Greenland in January of 1960. So in due course they packed up their belongings in the 1948 Henry J, the boy had purchased from the First Shirt, and headed for Clinton, Oklahoma and a brief leave before the boy had to leave for Greenland.

The leave allowed time to get Lucy settled with her parents for the duration of his deployment, and to get his mother-in-law's feelings soothed. This was required because Lucy was pregnant with their first child, so one more of the promises had been broken. This of course was the son-in-law's fault, so he was not a very popular individual with Lucy's family.

In due time the boy boarded a Grey Hound Bus at that station where he had first seen his Lucy and headed for McGuire Air Force Base in New Jersey and ultimately Thule, Greenland and a one year tour of duty 300 miles north of the Arctic Circle.

A MEMORY OR TWO OF THULE

Thule Greenland was a strange and enchanted land. Located some 300 miles north of the arctic circle most of the time it was either 24 hour daylight for months at a time or 24 hour darkness. The air was so dry it neither rained or snowed, unless the temperature began to rise above zero degrees Fahrenheit. As a matter of fact, the boy cannot remember it ever raining. However, he does remember the snow. When the temperature would begin to raise, warnings would be issued. These were called "phase warnings" and were numbered 1 through 5. Five being the worst.

This is a picture of the "dump" in March 1960 just shortly after the sun was up. It was located just east of the main base at Thule. It was filled with WWII era artillery guns and other assorted battle field equipment. Iconic Dundus mountain is in the back ground.

During the darkness period which lasted from mid October to mid March the boy cannot remember anything other than a phase one or two being called. When daylight poked its head up in the middle of March, over east mountain for a few minutes each day until it was fully up until October, the temps began their annual rise to above zero. It was then that the phase numbers began to clime. This usually resulted in strong winds, and the Ice Cap, loosing its hold on the top layer of snow that had been frozen from the air and deposited during the dark months.

The next series of pictures were taken after a Phase 4 moved through Thule in April just before the "Melt" began to take place and the snow began to disappear.

The boy remembers one phase five in late March which blew for 5 days. When it was over, they had to dig up six feet, to clear the barracks door to get out. There were four pickup trucks, two tractor trailers and a "Honey Bucket" truck buried in front of the building where they had been abandoned when their drivers took refuge in the barracks.

It took three days to get the roads cleared and the base back in operation. But vehicles and other buildings were still being dug out for a week after the storm ended. The actual snow fall was reported as zero, all the snow had been blown in from the Ice Cap.

The term "Honey Bucket" is the name used by all, for the tanker trucks that were used to collect all the waste fluids from the buildings. This was necessary since all of the structures were built over "Perma Frost" and no buried plumbing systems were possible. So, a truck was used which plugged into a special fire hydrant like fixture on each building on a regular schedule and drained the waste products from the tanks located inside the buildings. Likewise there were special water trucks that brought potable water and filled up storage tanks in each building.

Since water was always in short supply or the possibility of delayed refills was always a fact of life, water use was strictly monitored. One of the first instructions given upon arrival in Thule, concerned how to take a "Thule Shower". That is you stepped into the shower stall turned on the hot water first (hopefully without scalding yourself for it was always very hot), then turned on the cold water just long enough to get wet all over, then turned all the water off. You then soaped down and only turned on the cold water (never the hot), only long enough to rinse off. Punishment for taking to long in the shower was sever and quick. "Stateside Showers" were never allowed, ever! Also toilets were only allowed one flush and that used "grey water", that is recycled shower and sink water. You never let the water run when brushing your teeth or shaving.

The fixture outside the building where the "Honey Buckets" connected always seemed to leak a little when it was used. During the coldest months a frozen cone shaped deposit would form beneath it. As the uses and the weeks moved on this frozen mound would grow into what was affectionately known as a "Thule Popsicle". Not much of a problem during the frozen months and an effort was made to clear them before the summer thaw. However, since the summer thaw only lasted a few days in late July it was not a priority. One of the more pungent memories of Thule.

Another memory is of the vast open treeless landscape that presented itself as the sun rose. The boy remembers that the year he was there, the sun rose for five minutes on March 21st. It had presented itself for several days as a slightly less dark area over what was known as "east mountain". Oddly enough there was a small notch or pass in this mountain range, which appeared almost centered with the runway. It was in this notch that the sun made its first appearance to the boy. It rose exactly centered in this notch, until fully visible and then descended until fully obscured. This process repeated itself over the next few days until the sun remained up all the time, until in late October when it once more began to descend until it no longer cast its light or warmth over the land. The Arctic and Thule were dark once more.

There was a power ship moored alongside the pier in the bay. This supplied all the electrical power for the base. The heat generated by the generators kept the water and ice from forming around the ship. It was the only place were the Arctic Ocean was clear of ice and snow year round. The boy and many others would go there once in a while just to see this wonder. Occasionally someone would drop a fishing line into the water and most always catch a fish that looked like it was more bone and fins that any meat. As far as the boy knows they were always thrown back as inedible and somewhat frightening. Something from the dinosaur age it seemed.

The Ice Breakers finally broke the ice out of Dundas bay on July, 24th of that year, (this is remembered because that is his birthday),and kept it clear for the next two weeks. This allowed the supply ships to bring in the years supply of whatever was needed, but the item most remembered was, Beer, the base had ran out some two weeks earlier, and no one can take Thule completely sober.

The boy's room mate had sobered up a few days before he was due to ship stateside, and had gone off his trolley. He stole a staff car and proceeded to drive back to the states over the frozen ocean. The Air Police rescued him five miles out to sea, stuck on an ice flow. The staff car is still there or at the bottom of the ocean. He was shipped home on a hospital plane in a straight jacket. Our protagonist took that lesson to heart and sobered up over the Atlantic Ocean thirty minutes from landing at McGuire Air Force Base, New Jersey.

The strongest memory of Greenland and the one that became a catch phrase for the boy and probably for all who served there is this, "There were no women, no trees and no door knobs." Strangely enough it was the insignificant stateside comfort of a door knob which was missed the most, and which is still remembered to this day.

There is one other small memory that concerns the boys stay in Thule, and the soon to be born son. As with most couples naming the child forms the content of many conversations. The boy and his Lucy were no different in this process. They had long decided to continue the family tradition of the name "Kenneth", if the child was a boy, however, if the child should be a girl no such tradition existed, and there were no names that presented themselves as predominate enough for consideration. In due course, because of a WATTS phone call,(Lucy still misused the system), overheard by all the barracks, all of those living there joined in on the naming of the child, if it should be a girl. After much loud and rancorous discussion the name for a girl was declared to be "Vinora Flugot".

An Aside for the boy's son; "See how fortunate you were to not be born a female! You could have gone through life marked by a most unusual name. Hampered more to the truth."

Shortly before his tour was up the boy was called into the Executive Officers office,(second in command), to be given the "opportunity" to reenlist. The boy knew this was coming and was prepared for the "opportunity".

The Exec. asked him if he had considered whether or not he was going to re-up and the rest of the conversation went something like this.

"Yes Sir," he replied. "But I have three conditions, and I'd like them in writing, Sir." (This by the way is the only time any junior enlisted is ever allowed to propose conditions to a superior officer).

"And what might those be Linnell?" the Exec. asked with a gleam in his eye.

"Well Sir I'd like to have another stripe." "No problem at all, that you can have as soon as you sign up." "what else?"

Well Sir I'd like to go to a Tech. School and learn a trade."

"Well I don't see any problem there. What kind of School do you have in mind?"

"Well Sir I'm in the Air Force so I'd like something to do with Air Planes." He Replied.

"Well I believe we can find something to satisfy that condition without any problem. We can set it up so you would report directly to school at the end of your tour, when you return to the states. Now what is your third condition?"

"Well Sir I'd need you to guarantee I'll never come back to this damn place."

"You know damn well I can't do that. Get the hell out of my office and quit wasting my time!"

The boy thinks of that conversation often and is of the opinion that he was simply too full of "dumb" and the constant pestering of his wife to come home at that moment in time. He believes now that in the few moments of that conversation he made if not the biggest, certainly one of the largest mistakes of his life. However, it was made and on his return from Greenland the boy was honorably discharged and thus ended his military career.

⁂

He returned to Clinton, Oklahoma and his family. Their son Shane had been born in August, so the need for a job and all the responsibility of married life was there from the moment his feet touched the ground in the United States. He quickly realized that no training, combined with no education meant jobs of low pay, short duration, and hard work. Yet, life with Lucy was sweet and the couple were happy in their life with their son.

As in any marriage there were good times and other times. Lucy gave him three children, Shane, Tina and Daina. The best and sweetest part of the marriage. As in any relationship there are many stories and memories that could be told, but they will not be told here. They belong in the file marked, "to be shared by husband and wife only." It is enough to say that our boy loved Lucy with everything he could muster, and understood to be love.

However, some where along the way, Lucy was replaced with Mildred, and she, he did not like at all. However, when "Millie" showed up even Mildred headed for the hills. So after ten years and three more of legal battles, he threw in the towel and called it quits. It was a decision which did not come easy to our protagonist, because he had always vowed his children would not grow up without a father., yet, to his great sorrow they did.

It must be said here that in all of the years that have followed, and now in the winter of his years when he thinks of that portion of his life, it is Lucy, he chooses to remember. She was his first true love and he believes that if Mildred had not come to replace Lucy, they would never have been separated. At least that is the dream, but life moves on in spite of ones dreams.

The divorce took three years to be proclaimed by the courts. It was not the slowness of the Oklahoma court system, but rather "Mildred and Millie" that caused the seemingly endless delays. In the end "Millie's" lawyer paid her to sign the final decree in order to get her off his back. The boy, (our hero) breathed a sigh of relief, believing that at last he could move on into something of a normal life.

But that was not to be, for "Millie" or "Mildred" he never knew which, kept finding new lawyers, and every month for the next two years he was served with parers to appear in court. These papers were usually given to him by a Sheriff's deputy, waiting at the house, when he appeared for his monthly visitation with the children.

Finally in 1974 the judge told "Mildred" he had grown sick and tired of seeing her in his court every month and that if she ever filed another harassing motion against the boy, he would put her in jail for contempt of court and wasting the courts time and resources. He instructed her to pay all the costs for that case. He then turned to the boy and said, "Son, take my advice and run for the hill's. Courts dismissed."

There never was another court case filed, but the harassment continued in many different forms. Finally in the fall or winter of 1983 she finally gave up.

However, long before then, due to misinformation, innuendo, and misunderstanding, any amicable contact with the children had been lost. This was due mostly to a couple of factors which need to be addressed.

In any break up of a marriage and family there is always more than enough blame to be shared. First is the responsibility of the two "adults" involved in the breakup. Each shares in more than enough reasons, all of which could and do start wars among nations.

In this case both were equally at fault. Mildred in her compulsion to rule the world and everything in it. Our protagonist, (ME), because of all the reasons piled upon him from the moment of his father's death, until that point in his life at the ripe old age of thirty something, when he just couldn't take anymore. Rather than stand up to the situation, he simply melted into the background, always there but never present.

The children in their young years were effected the most and bear the deepest scars. This is I believe, because in their youthful understandings and misunderstandings, they arrived at decisions for which they were not prepared. They accepted blame at times for circumstances and reasons, which were not, nor could never be their fault. They also assigned blame, when their information was incorrect, or simply colored too strongly by their own youthful understandings, sorrow and anger.

Also there was a factor involved which had been placed over their lives, which had its beginnings that January night in 1945 when their father had stood on the landing, watched and listened, as his mother was told her husband, and his father had been killed.

This single event set into motion life changing events in the lives of the boy and his brothers. Events which by their very nature prevented these young boys, and the adults they became, from knowing how to be "normal".

As a result in this case, when the breakup of this young family occurred, there were expectations placed upon the boy, for which he had no comprehension of solution. He simply did not know how to be "normal".

Now in the winter of his years, many estrangements still exist, largely because of his simply not knowing how to meet the expectations. Also because those who hold those expectations cannot release them or have no conception of the need for release. This process requires the awareness and acknowledgment, that the father, in reality never was as they thought him to be, and an acceptance of his defects.

As a result there are children that are now adults who didn't have a father, grandfather, great grandfather, and god help us great great grand children possibly. Those years have passed and can never be recovered. Probably our protagonist's deepest sorrow is this one thing, along with the knowledge that even now, there are still expectations that can never be resolved, because he just simply does not know how.

Some, a few have been resolved, something that took years, in one case to rectify, and in others is still a work in progress. Thankfully that process still continues.

PART II.A

Adulthood on Hold

(in order to fill in a few blanks)

EDUCATION
(BETTER LATE THAN NEVER)

A brief explanation is required at this point. Upon his separation from the Air Force as mentioned earlier, the boy realized he was in for a very difficult life if he didn't obtain some kind of training and education. Since he had never finished High School any higher education was out of the question. After many false starts he found a training program through the Oklahoma Employment Service and received schooling as an auto mechanic. After completing the course he was able to gain steady employment at a reasonably good rate of pay and for the first time in their lives together the boy and Lucy felt prosperous. They had disposable income that allowed them to add some comforts and luxuries into the family lifestyle.

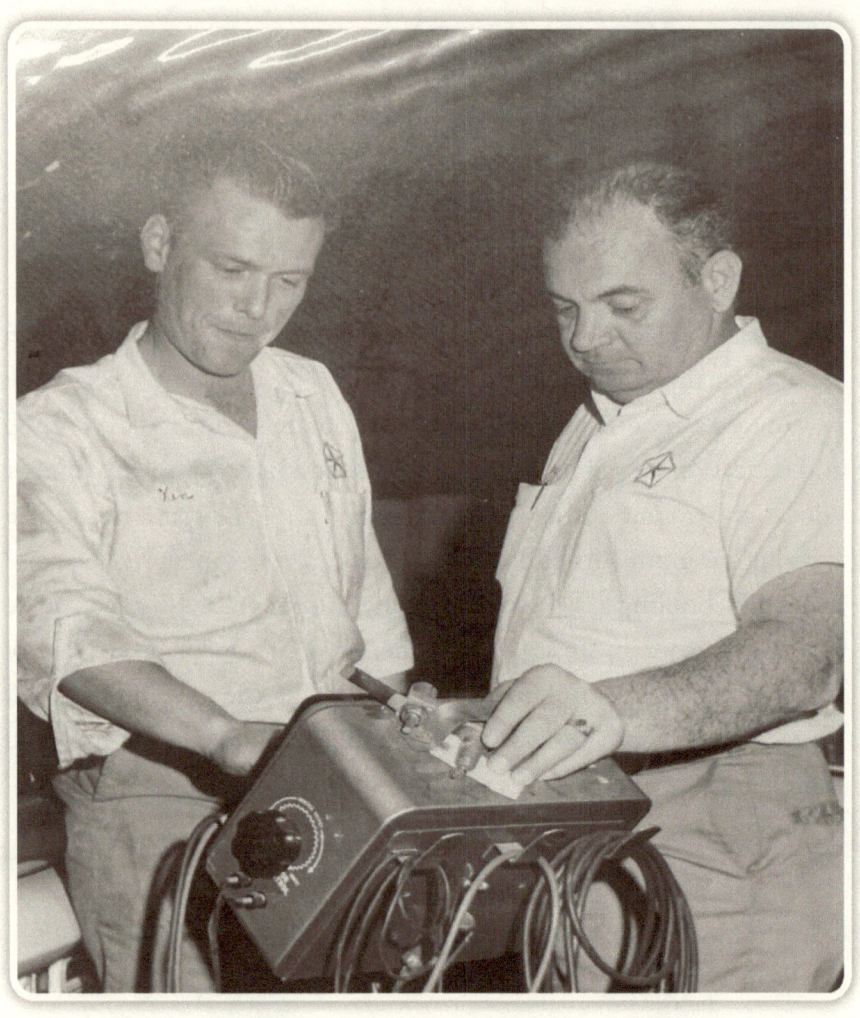

Me on the left during my Auto Mechanic school days

During the summer of 1965 the young family lived a few miles west of Oklahoma City and the boy worked for a Chrysler dealership on the north west side of town. Because of some on going training requirements of his job he became aware of Oklahoma State University Technical Collage located in Oklahoma City.

Upon checking into some classes he learned this was actually more of a JR. College than a Tech. School and was about to write it off because he hadn't finished school and didn't have a GED. He told the enrollment officer this and was told that in Oklahoma if you were over twenty one, a resident of the state for a required number of years, (don't remember how many), and could pass the entrance exam. you didn't have to have a high school diploma, or a GED. You could enroll at any State supported collage or university. The only requirement was that you had to maintain a three point average over the courses taken for the first semester, (with no set number of courses that had to be taken during that qualifying semester). After that you were just like everyone else.

This was music to the boy's ears. He immediately scheduled the entrance exam, and sweated bullets while he prepared for the exam, and waited for the day to arrive. Then he sweated blood while he took the exam, and waited in the student commons, area after the exam for the results.

He doesn't remember his score and it is not important because he passed!

He immediately enrolled in two classes which he was told were an easy "A" and launched his educational career with the help of the G.I. Bill. His time in the Air Force turned out to be a big help after all.

In the fall of 1966 he transferred to the University of Oklahoma School of Architecture, Norman, Oklahoma. It was a five year program with graduation anticipated in the spring of 1972, however, because of several factors, not the least of which was he married life with, "Mildred", and his family responsibilities, he did not receive his graduation and diploma until 1974.

With the disintegration of his family the boy left the University and moved to Dallas, Texas, as far as he could at the time, live and still see the kid's occasionally. The boy was working at an Architectural firm in Dallas Texas, and had been enabled by the assistant Dean of the Architectural School to complete the degree requirements by correspondence.

Many years later in 2001 he enrolled at Emory University, Chandler School of Theology in Atlanta, Georgia. Graduating in 2003 with a Master of Divinity Degree.

In 2005 he began classes in the Doctoral Program at The King's College and Seminary, Van Nuys, California. Graduating in 2008 with an earned Doctorate in Ministry.

GRANDMOTHERS

Most people have two Grandmothers. My Children only ever had one. However I have three. I shall do my best to tell of them, so that they will not be completely lost to the vagaries of time and history, but in some small fashion live on in the minds and memories of their great grand children and the generations that follow them.

Since they have been gone from this realm for a great distance of time and I am the only remaining soul who knows of them I see no need for anonymity so I will name them here at least by the names known to me and in the order of appearance in my life.

First there is my fathers mother, Clara Lindsay

I never met this lady as she died in the Spanish flu epidemic in 1919-20 if my memory serves me. However, my fathers brother told me of her and those facts I will recite here.

She was born in Prophets Town Illinois after her parents moved north from southern Tennessee to escape the ravages of the Civil War. Though they lived in the south they were not sympathetic with the Southern cause. Her father was an emigrant from Scotland arriving here as a young man when his family immigrated prior to the war beginning.

She was a slender smallish woman with a dark complication and high cheek bones. Because of this some have decided that she was Native American. This, however, is simply not the case. She was a true Scott. Her looks and features were passed on to her through the Pict ancestry of the land of her fathers.

She traveled with her parents by wagon train from Illinois to north central Kansas. They settled in an area of the Republican River valley of Northern Kansas where Joseph Linnell and his family settled and were awarded a homestead on March,10 1890. It was here that she met and married Seth Linnell and in the progress of time she gave birth to two sons. Kenneth Alvin Linnell and Seth Eldred Linnell.

Around the turn of the century she moved with her husband and two boys to Kansas City where there was plenty of work and the family could prosper. It was here that she contracted the Spanish flu and died.

My father died when I was very young so there is no recollection of his memories of his mother.

It is to this woman's credit, however, that her youngest son, my uncle BO as he was known, remembers her fondly, and though the members of our family are very close with their emotions, he always spoke of her with a great deal of love some fifty years after her death, as he told me of her.

I was told that my Grandfather was very much at a loss at her passing and moved back to the family homestead with his two sons, where there was his mother and family to help him raise his family. It was during this period that he met and married grand mother number two.

Seth T and Clara Lindsay Linnell in 1910. Father's parents.

Seth and Clara Linnell with son's
Kenneth (left) and Eldred "Uncle Bo. (right)

Eldred, Uncle Bo (left) Kenneth, the authors father (Right)

Second there is my fathers step mother, Margret O'Brian.

I know nothing of this ladies origins, though they most certainly were Irish. I first became aware of her in 1946 when my brothers and I were sent to live with our Uncle Bo. Uncle Bo was single at that time and having just returned from the war in Europe lived with his fathers family. As our guardian he was saddled with us, by our mother, at a time which could only have been most inconvenient for my Grandfather and his second wife.

Grandfather had homesteaded a farm north and west of Goodland, Kansas before the depression years. During the war years to make it more convenient for their children to attend school in the winter, the family had moved into Goodland, purchasing a house on Walnut St. It was here that I remember first meeting GrandMa Linnell as she was called.

After their marriage, there were five living children added to the family, so there were seven children in GrandMa Linnell's household seven boys/men and three girls/women.

When my brothers a I came to live at the house on Walnut street, there were still four of these remaining at home the youngest was 15 years of age. So with the addition of myself and my brothers there once again were seven children in the house. My grandfather was ill and in the hospital often, which added to the burden of having to care once more for three young ones. At that time six, four and three years of age. It is to her credit, that she, with the help of her two youngest daughters cared for us.

Our Uncle Bo, was mostly always working, and because of his war years drank a lot, so we didn't see much of him. The older boys also were busy on the family farm and at school during the winter, there was also little contact with them.

I remember GrandMa Linnell as a rather stout woman. Not fat, but stout, and of course from the view point to a six year old, very tall. Though she was not much above five feet tall. My memories of adults in that period of my life is that every one was gigantic.

GrandMa Linnell's hair was always drawn back and tied in a bun, and she always had the smell about her of fresh baked bread. Probably because she baked everyday of her life except Sunday, when she always attended church at the First Methodist Church. She always baked double on Saturday to make up for it.

She was not a friendly or loving woman, however, she kept her family clean, fed and clothed. Which now with the passing of time I can see was probably all she had time to do. I do remember that she was very attentive to Grandfather. That portion of her life was removed from the rest of the family. Grandfather resided in the bed room on the side of the house which connected directly to the large kitchen and family room. But this area was off limits to the young children. Grandfather rarely made an appearance with the family.

There were two occasions when my brothers and I were foisted upon GrandMa Linnell's family the first as I mentioned was when we suddenly arrived in Kansas after living in Kuna, Idaho which had to have been in late 1947. That ended when my mother settled in California and we went to live with her and her new family. The second was in 1950 when our mother died and my brothers and I were sent back to live with our fathers family, or what remained of it.

When we arrived in Kansas once more in 1950, nothing much had changed. The family farm had been sold. And the older boys were off to collage or the military. The two youngest daughters were still at home, but the oldest soon married. My Grand father passed way shortly after we arrived in Goodland the second time. So all that remained was the youngest daughter. GrandMa Linnell had gotten a little shorter, mostly because I had gotten a little taller, however, she was still stern and unloving as ever. We had arrived in January and we were carted of to live with our mothers parents in Idaho that spring.

And so began our lives with Grandmother number three, Lona Bell Mercer.

While the boy lived with this grandmother for some six years between 1950 and 1956 there is not much he can say about her. This is a shame, for everyone deserves to have their story known. Therefore an attempt will be made to tell something of this women. Most of these details were given to him years after her passing by one of mothers sisters just before she also passed.

She was born and raised in part in northwestern Arkansas some time shortly after the turn of the century. The family was large as was normal in those times. At some point before her fourteenth birthday the family moved from the area of Bentonville, Arkansas to a farm near Claremore, Oklahoma.

The story goes that the family made this move because she had gotten involved with a "Gentry" boy, who her father and mother considered to be a very bad influence, not the sort they wished for their daughter. This "Gentry" boy was some years older at 18 and at the time of the move she was only a few days past of her thirteenth birthday.

Apparently, aided by one of her sisters, the relationship was continued in secret by mail. A few days before her fourteenth birthday, again aided by this same sister she, ran away from home and met the "Gentry" boy at the train depot in Claremore, Oklahoma.

All of this had been prearranged through the mail. The couple then traveled by train to Russellville, Arkansas to the home of one of the "Gentry" boy's brother. There on her fourteenth birthday Lona Bell Mercer became Lona Bell Gentry the wife of LaBanual Anderson Gentry. Her Parents were only informed after the wedding. The story says that she never saw her parents again as they completely disowned her for her actions. The veracity of this fact is not known. However, it is known that she only learned of their passing years later through a sister who moved to Boise Idaho. This was many years after they had passed.

At the time of our protagonist's association with "Grandma" Gentry she was in her early fifties and seemed very old to him. By this time she had given birth to nine babies with eight serving. Her life had up to that point in time been consumed with raising this brood while living and working on a share-croppers farm. Also surviving the Great Depression and World War Two. She spent pretty much every day of her life tied to household drudgery or working in the fields. She cared for her family and spent her life literally insuring their survival. Now in the winter of his years he believes she had every right to seem old.

He remembers her as a rather cold person. She didn't laugh much. There never was a hug. However, every morning there was a great big farm breakfast waiting for everyone, as well as a large hot meal in the evening, after the chores were done.

Her one vice was that she dipped snuff, "Garrett's Snuff" to be exact. She always had an empty "Clabber Girl" baking powder can nearby in to which she spit. There also usually was a small dribble of snuff on her chin, which didn't make it into the baking powder can.

She appeared to worship her husband beyond all reason. In the years the boy lived in the house with Grandma and Grandpa Gentry he does not remember a harsh word ever being spoken between the two. They truly lived their lives as one. However, this resulted in the exclusion of all others.

Her children, those he knew during those years, all seemed to love their mother in particular. However, they all, when they reached an age where they could, left home, with most never returning. During those years the boy cannot remember his mother ever being mentioned in any fashion at all.

Grandma Gentry never spoke of the children who had gone on with their lives in other parts of the world, even the two who lived in

Nampa. However, when an occasional letter would appear from one of her distant children, she would carry it in a pocket of her apron for weeks, after it had been read to her. She could read a little, but with difficulty, so usually the youngest of the boy's mother's sisters, Shirley would read the letters to her. The boys remembers Grandma sitting in her rocking chair in the large kitchen, rocking slowly with her eyes closed, with a smile on her face, as she listened to the letters. It is the only time he remembers her smiling.

There are a large number of stories concerning these women that have been lost forever. They have all gone on to their reward in the other life. All three were strong believers in Christ Jesus and I believe they are with him now. They were from a very different generation than most of us, even of the Boy. Their's was a generation of hard work simply to survive. A generation of great sacrifice, unknown to the generations they precede. Largely because of this they were seen by their following generation as hard, cold and unloving. However, just possibly if the stories that are lost forever, could be known they would be seen in an entirely different light.

PART II.B

Children

Children, what can be said about children that has not already been said a thousand times over. However, since this is a collection of memories from the life of one individual an effort will be made to speak of the children of this life.

THE SON

Shane

The boy's first born is a son, Kenneth Shane, born in Clinton, Oklahoma on August 13th, 1960. Our boy was just past his twentieth birthday. The boy was present at his birth, at least at the hospital, fathers were not allowed into the delivery rooms in those days. The child's statistics are not remembered, but he was a large baby.

The boy was still in the Air Force at the time and stationed in Thule Greenland. He was able to be at the birth because Mildred had harassed the Red Cross and the Air Force authorities so much, one Red Cross worker had told the Air Force officials, if they didn't get this women of his back he was going to kill himself. The result was the boy was given an emergency leave, unceremoniously put on the first available aircraft departing Thule and shipped back to the states for thirty days.

Adjectives used to describe new born babies are usually, pretty, cute, even beautiful. They are most often used in declarative statements by women other than the mother such as, "Oh isn't he so cute," or "Oh my how hansom he is!"

Has any one ever wondered why the men are silent on this subject, responding only when there is no other choice with something like, "Mighty fine looking boy you got there."? Most likely it's because the lens of the male eye see's a different picture than that of the female eye.

To our protagonist, while he felt very deep emotions of pride, protection, and even possibly love, the child before him was not much more than a rather large shriveled pink worm, which seemed to explode with large smelly messes, from both ends at regular intervals.

The fact is he knew under threat of pain and a swift, sudden, and painful death, he could not state these observations within the hearing of his wife or his mother-in-law. So, he also, when forced responded with platitudes such as, "He sure is a Big'un!" etc. etc. Largely, because of this, he was grateful to once more crawl on to a bus and head for the peace and quite of Thule Greenland.

Upon our protagonists permanent return to the states and separation from the Air Force a few months later, his son had moved from being a shriveled up worm to something more substantial who did not seem to care for his father very much. A condition that lasted until the child began to move around on its own and more closely resembled a human child.

Then and for some time to come, where ever our hero was, so was his son if at all possible. When the boy wasn't at work, his son was glued to his leg. Literally at times. The child thought it great fun to sit on his fathers foot, wrapping his little arms and legs tightly around his fathers leg, riding there until some other need interceded forcing him to let go.

The boy cannot remember when his son began to talk or walk it seems as if he always did. He does remember it was a sad day when his son grew to be to big to ride on his fathers leg, wherever they roamed.

As with all children you turn around and one day they are large, complete autonomous being. Maybe not full grown, yet with lives and feeling of their own. It seems the adults are always surprised by this event, however, none the less it happens.

Like all adults, a term loosely used, the boy was so caught up in making a living and providing for his family, so one day he turned and there before him stood his son. Not yet grown, but complete with his own set of needs, likes and dislikes, a complete individual. A proud day for our protagonist but a sad one because he realized in that moment that there was a lot of his son's life to that point he had missed.

The boy does not have many memories of his son in his childhood. Of course the divorce from his mother at the child's young age accounts for some of that.

There is a picture of our protagonist holding his son. In this picture the boy is dressed in western style clothes. That is boots, jeans, a western style shirt and a stetson style hat. He is also wearing a gun belt complete with pistol. He is standing in the back yard of his in-laws's home holding his son. The child cannot be more that several months to a year old. There are no memories of when this picture was taken but the boy believes it must have been taken shortly after his return from Greenland.

There is a memory of his son coming into the house where they lived just prior to the breakup. He came through the door with three or four other boys from the neighborhood. They rushed through the living room with Shane saying "Hi Dad" as they rushed to his room to look for something and then just as quickly back the way they had came and out the door to the yard.

Most of the memories of his son are tied up with his sister Tina. From the moment Tina exited from the "pink worm" category the two were inseparable. They were best friends as well as brother and sister.

DAUGHTER #1

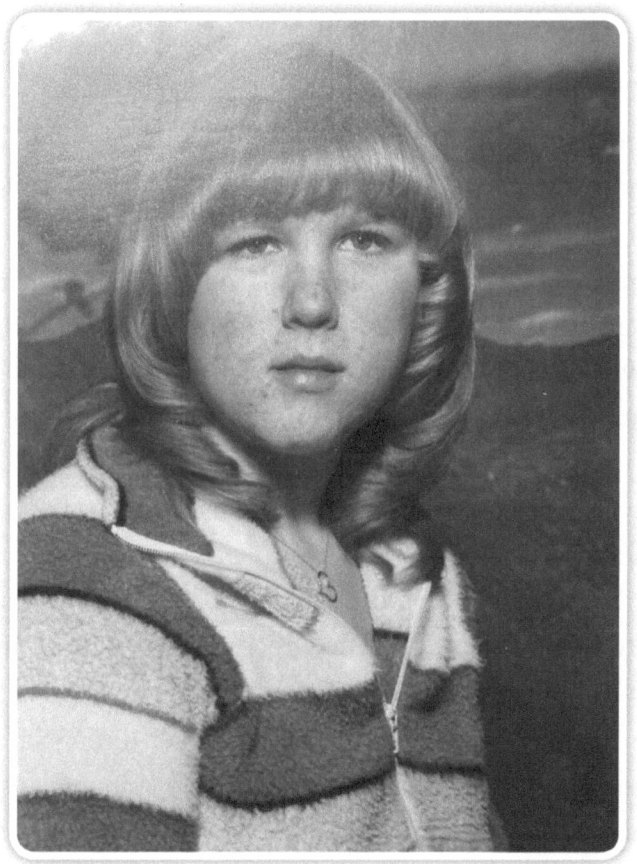

Tina

Tina Waynett was born March, 29th, 1962 in Bremerton Washington. Our young father was some four months short of his twenty second birthday. Once again the boy was present, waiting in a long semi dark hall way, because fathers were not allowed in the delivery rooms. He waited for what seemed hours, however, the length of time is unknown. He had arrived home that morning from his job as a night watchman in Seattle. He had walked from the ferry terminal the two miles or so to his home, he didn't have a car. He was immediately informed by Lucy as he entered the door, she was still Lucy in those days, that it was time and she had to get to the hospital, NOW!

The boy called his Aunt Bernice, one of mothers sisters, and within 15 minutes they were at the hospital.

Once again, as he looked upon his new born daughter, all he could see was a rather chubby, but cute pink worm. The boys sense of judgment was improving with age.

There are not many memories of Tina separate from her brother. They were always together from her first moments crawling around on her own. When she stood up and took her first step her second step was running after her brother. It was as if the two were Siamese twins.

The two of them were always wrestling, running after one another, laughing. In general making enough noise to wake the whole house, except when they were sleeping. Even then they had to be in the same room or they would not "settle" down. Only when they were in the same room where they could see each other would they finally go to sleep.

One memory of Tina is of her being led through the Seattle train station after returning from a trip to Oklahoma. As the boy remembers it, his first sight of her was of a very pretty toddler dressed in a rather heavy blue woolen suit with a matching hat. It was late in July and a very hot day.

The poor child was severely uncomfortable, yet, when she saw her father, her face lit up like a candle. She was all smiles for her father. When questioned about Tina's attire her mother informed the boy that Tina had came down with a case of the measles after they had departed Oklahoma. Her mother had dressed her that way so when questioned she could explain away the red face, perspiration etc as heat rash. Her brother was also attached to her hand as she was thrust into her fathers arms with," here it's your turn now!"

The measles would depart in due course, however, as soon as they got into the car that day the wool clothes came off. There was no air conditioner in the car, but Tina was placed as close as her father and her brother could get her to the wing vent of the passenger side door so that the breeze would cool her down.

There are memories of the family traveling together in whatever automobile they had at the moment. The boy and Lucy would sit in the front with Tina and her brother in the back. This was pre- car seat and seat belt days, so the result was always a wrestling match in the back seat. Nothing mean or hurtful, just a brother and sister who for at least the first eight or ten years of their lives absolutely adored each other. When they were together they were the center of each others world.

There was a constant comment from the adults in the front seat, usually from the boy, that went something like this, "If you two don't behave back there I'm going to stop the car and tan both of your backsides until you can't sit down!" He never stopped and neither did they.

There was one time, however, when the family was headed somewhere when our gallant father gave them a couple of swift licks just before they got into the car. Telling them, "this is in advance for what I know your going to do. Now behave." It was a little quieter that time, but to say they behaved would be putting it to strong.

It has always been Tina's lot to have been the second child and eventually the middle child. Memory's of her separate from her siblings are hard to bring to focus. There are fragments of memories of a beautiful little girl with strawberry blond hair. A few freckles scattered across rosy cheeks and with a big smile across her face.

However, those fragments are always broken up as another memory of her running after her big brother takes it s place.

DAUGHTER #2

Daina

Daina Ruth was born on December 26, 1964 in Clinton, Oklahoma. Our boy was some six months past his twenty fifth birthday. The Boy was again present for the birth of his third child. However, once again not allowed anywhere close to the delivery room. The wait was long and complicated by his father-in-law coming and going because he was on duty as an officer in the Clinton police force. Also the fact that the boy was still not his favorite person in the world. In due course as they say, Daina made her appearance into the world and finally the boy was allowed to see his newest child. He remembers her as a slender, somewhat shriveled pink worm. However, he also remembers thinking, she was a rather pretty pink worm. His sensibilities had improved a great deal with a little age.

This little girl was some thing different. This is often said about Christmas babies, yet in this case it is true.

She began to crawl very early and to pull herself up soon after, but she could not stand up yet without support. Her older brother and sister claimed her almost immediately upon her arrival home from the hospital. As soon as she was mobile they were constantly helping her to stand or just playing with her on the floor. Yet, he remembers they never played as rough with her as they did with each other. There is a picture of the three of them standing on the front porch looking at their father in the car. Daina is in the middle being supported by her older brother ans sister. This was always they way it was for them.

Daina could never seem to learn to walk. When she was around eighteen months old, just about the time the picture just mentioned was taken, it was learned that she had a condition called, "Bilateral Congenital Dislocated Hips". This is doctor speak to say her hip sockets had not formed properly. In her case one of her hips had no socket at all and the other had only a slight hint of one. Because of this it was impossible for her legs to support her body. This was the reason she had never been able to walk.

This news brought on a very difficult time in the life of the boy's young family. An operation was needed and it was a very costly process. How, where etc etc.

There never was a question in the boy's mind, but that his daughter was going to get what she needed. He was no matter what it took going to see to it that she had every shot at living as full and as normal a life as possible.

Over the next several weeks there were many conferences with doctor's, insurance companies, and hospitals. Eventually it was determined that she would have her surgery at a hospital in Oklahoma City associated with the University of Oklahoma Medical School.

Our boy also was, told that the process was to be long and at times difficult. So the decision was made for him to get a job in Oklahoma City so that he could be near by and be able to visit his daughter during her weeks in the hospital.

The final meeting with the doctor, just prior to Daina being admitted to the hospital is forever etched in the boy's mind. Our protagonist, Lucy and Grandmother James, (Lucy's grandmother), were in the large public waiting area of the hospital waiting for the doctor to arrive. Lucy and her grandmother were debating the necessity of the surgery, continually back and forth, and largely the boy was ignoring them, watching his daughter as she played with the toys in the waiting room.

As he remembers that morning, he had not said more than a word or two to anyone, and he was not being included in the conversation going on between his wife and her grandmother. Finally the doctor came out and began speaking to Lucy and her grandmother mostly, with the boy listening closely to everything being said.

In brief the doctor was telling the two women that without the surgery Daina would never walk. Ultimately she would be confined to a wheel chair and would have to learn how to manage a great deal of pain through out her life. He said that Daina would never be able to live a normal life and could never have children, if she did not have the surgery. He stated, that if she had the surgery there was an eighty percent chance she would be able to live a normal life, and be able to do anything she wanted to do.

He also said that everything was ready, all the doctors, surgery schedules, insurance, all the things necessary for something like this to take place had been done. All that remained was for one of her parents to sign the permission slip.

The boy could not believe what he heard, Grandmother James spoke up and said," Well we believe in prayer and divine healing, and just don't know if this is really necessary." Lucy Spoke up and said, "I am just not sure about this, I think I need to go back home and talk to my father about this. I'll be in touch later."

The doctor stood before them in stunned unbelief for a moment. Only a moment, because The boy, Daina's father, stepped forward and said rather loudly, "I'm her father and I'll sign that damn paper right now!" He then turned on Grandmother James and spoke the first and only unkind words he had ever spoken to that lady, he told her, as she was protesting his actions, that Daina was his daughter and she had no say in what was happening and it was also none of her damn business what he did or didn't do.

Lucy, or rather it should be said Mildred, came at him with all her claws and fangs, telling him at the top of her voice, that she was going to decide what happened to her daughter not him.

For the first time in their married life the boy looked into the face of his wife and told her to sit down and shut up. The decision had been made and the papers had been signed. It was going to happen.

The doctor smiled, turned to the boy and said, "You've made the right decision son. Admitting is ready as soon as you go over there.

Mildred stated," well if your going to do this your going to do it on your own". She then gathered up her things, her grandmother and left the hospital, loaded up into the family car and returned to Clinton to tell her father just what his least favorite son-in-law had done.

It must be said here that when she did tell her father what the boy had done, and what she had done, it is the only time the boy can remember when his father-in-law backed him up. Telling his rather shocked daughter, the boy had done the right thing and she better accept it.

The boy never knew what he told her exactly, or what he had told Grandmother James, but he never heard another word about it from either one of them.

Daina was checked into the hospital and over the next couple of weeks had surgeries on both her hips. She emerged from the hospital several weeks later wearing a full body cast from her armpits down to the souls of her feet. Her legs were held apart by a rod built into the cast at the bottom of her feet, at approximately a sixty degree angle. There was an opening at her groin area were a diaper could be inserted and her legs were twisted into slightly strange angles to her body. This was done, he was told, to help hold the bone graphs forming the new hip sockets in place until they grew together. She wore this cast and it's replacements for the following twenty months or so of her life.

There are several memories of those months while Daina was in the hospital and her recovery at home wearing that god awful, yet, wonderful cast.

The boy got a new job as a mechanic for the Chrysler dealership on May Avenue, in Oklahoma City. He spent his week days at work, his evenings at the hospital with Daina, even though she would not have anything to do with him. She had decided, he had deserted her and she would not even look at him for several weeks. But, he went every evening except Saturday, when he had to work until ten and on Sunday evening when he was driving back from Clinton. During these weeks he stayed with Lucy's uncle J. F. and his family who lived close by.

Eventually the family moved to the Oklahoma City area and Daina after several weeks was released from the hospital. Still in her cast, but by that time everyone including her siblings, were accustomed to it.

The biggest problem was that she was immobile. That is the cast was so big and heavy she was simply stuck were ever she was placed. This was not a condition she was ready to accept so either the boy or her mother was constantly moving her around the house, so she could be part of what ever her brother and sister had going on at the moment.

The solution came when a neighbor off offhandedly remarked that the cast should have come with roller skates. A light bulb went off and shortly thereafter Daina was equipped with a plywood board cut to match her cast. Attached to the underside of this board were several sets of wheels.

The board was a "V" shaped contraption, with the narrow end cut to fit under her chest as she was laying down . This kept her upper body and arms free. The wider end was cut to fit the cast and the angle of her feet so that she was secure.

In just a few moments after she was placed on this contraption she was off and running. The house was a medium size three bed room with tiled floors in every room. There was no where in the house she could not go, and she went everywhere. Even though she was bound to this very awkward cast for months, she was part of the family just as any child crawling around their home. Occasionally she would get stuck, but either her brother or her sister seemed to always be there, to give the extra push to get her going again.

It is unknown by the boy if either of her siblings remember much about this time, but their father has always been very proud and amazed by the way they cared for their sister during that difficult time in her life.

Eventually the cast came off and at somewhere just past three and a half years old Daina took her first steps. To her fathers knowledge she has never stopped since. As the doctor predicted many years ago she has led a full and normal life. The boy has never ever regretted standing up to Grandmother James and Mildred on that day so long ago.

DAUGHTER #3

Amanda

Amanda Kathleen was born in Irving, Texas on May 2nd, 1972 Our boy was some five months away from his thirty third birthday. The boy was present for the birth of his forth child and was yet again barred from the delivery room. (*It is commonly portrayed by Hollywood and the film industry that fathers are always in the delivery room cheering on the mother. It is also considered by many to be the case in hospitals* and so on that this is true in real life. However, I must say I doubt it, and am very grateful to never been allowed into that particular space.) The boy has no memory of his daughter shortly after her birth. If she was a shriveled pink worm, he is unaware. She could even have been cute or pretty, however if she was, there is still no memory.

Those were troubled times. There was constant hassle from Mildred, with the court, and the Sheriff, as well as anything else she could dream up. It was a time when the older two children and eventually even Daina decided to forgo the visits with their father.

Amanda was normal in every way a child is normal and she grew up surrounded with love and attention, largely from her maternal grandparents, who thought their first grandchild was gold plated.

The boy and her mother were determined that she should have a normal childhood and for the first six or so years she did.

From the time Amanda was about three years old the family lived in the country, near Guthrie, Oklahoma. She grew up around farm animals and pets. There were always dogs and cats as well as a menagerie of farm animals.

One memory is of her standing by the fence singing to three steers as they munched their hay. She stopped and asked her father, who was busy building a rabbit hutch, if he could make her a "mikey phone" like she had seen on T.V.. The boy looked at her kind of puzzled for a moment and then picked up a small piece of 2x2 and whittled out a shape similar to a microphone. He fastened a short piece of clothes line rope to the handle, handed it to his little girl, and asked if that would do? She smiled a big smile and said "Thank you Daddy!" She then turned with the "mikey phone" in her hand, stepped up on to the little stool she carried everywhere, placed the "mikey phone" up to her mouth, and once more sang her serenade to the steers.

Another memory of Amanda is of her sitting in a little lawn chair, just her size, with her pet nanny goat "Pennut Butter" laying beside her. She was singing into her "mikey phone" as she stroked and petted her pet goat with the other hand.

⌘

What has been written here seems a paltry amount of words to express the stories of the lives of at least the four people briefly mentioned here as the children. However, it seems to be enough for these few words if viewed closely will be found to express in its fullness the love, pride and joyous wonder of a father who wonders how he could have been so blessed, yet be found so wanting at the same time.

As in all things the children all have grown up and now have children and even grandchildren of their own. Maybe some day one of them will read this and then just possibly they will also have memories of the parents or grandparents, they never had before. Maybe just possibly, even of a grandfather, or great grandfather they never knew they had.

Possibly also even a father.

PART II.C

Adulthood Resumed

The years from the time of the separation in 1971 until 1979 were taken up with attempting to build a career in the Architectural world and attempts at building some kind of life that included his children. There were some successes and failures. Mostly failures.

∞

Also during those years there were several "Almost Wives" and one actual wife.

Shortly after the divorce was final in 1972 the boy married Lana. He had met her during the "legal years" as they were known in polite society.

Lana was married when they met and so was our protagonist, even though he had removed himself from the marriage with Mildred, he was still married. They began an affair which soon resulted in Lana leaving her husband and moving out on her own.

The two of them, our boy and Lana, on two occasions even moved in together. The first was halted by an insane judge, who ordered the boy to move back in with his family, or face an eternity in jail for contempt. The first of many such idiotic judgments Mildred was able to wrangle from the court system with her winning smile, down cast eyes, and Madonna like pleadings.

The second was terminated when the boy took a job with an Architectural firm in Dallas, Texas, as a means of escape, and moved to Dallas. The affair did not end, however, but continued as a long distance relationship until the divorce was ultimately final and they married.

It was not a match made in heaven, but then it is believed that none are. Relationships take a lot of work. Some are worth it, others aren't.

This marriage produced one child, a daughter, who was named Amanda.

There were a lot of struggles, but the two genuinely liked one another. Also between their previous marriages and divorces, they had been through a lot together. Thus allowing them to form a bond which held the marriage together for some seven years, in spite of the continual issues from past relationships.

Finally in 1979 the relationship was found to be no longer worth the work, and the marriage ended, not unexpectedly, but never the less with pain and sorrow.

A word about the almost wives. Over the years there were several. They were women who came along at various times in the boys life when there was a gap which needed filling. It is not accounted against them that they never made the status of "wife". Frankly, perhaps it was their good fortune that they never gained such exalted status.

They were all loving and warm and with the exception of one are remembered warmly. They will not be pictured here in this collection of memories for it is felt this is not the place for them to be displayed. It is enough to say they are there and are remembered.

PART III

The Rest of the Story

AWAKENING

Earlier in these pages there was a recalling of a journey across the North West Kansas country side by the boy and his family. In later years the boy learned that most likely this event occurred on a Sunday as his father and the family journeyed either to or from a country Methodist Church were his father was the Lay Minister, (The term used in those days. Now the title is Local Pastor). As the boy learned his fathers dream was to attend Seminary in Denver, Colorado and become an Elder and full time Pastor serving the Methodist church and the people of Northern Kansas where he was raised. To this end father had secured a position as Fireman on the Rock Island Railroad, a good paying steady job in the years following the Great Depression. His goal was to save enough money to afford seminary and to provide for his family while there.

When the United States was drawn into World War II in December of 1941, fathers position at the railroad was considered as essential to the war effort and he was not allowed to enlist in the military, but required to remain at his job for the duration. He therefore, was spared going off to war with his brother and for the first time in their adult lives the two were separated.

This was a double edged sword for the boys father, he was told years later by some who had known his father well. While he was able to remain at home and provide and care for his family, he also had to remain behind as his beloved brother went off into danger.

Those who knew father well told the boy that his father was a deeply devote and devoted man. While not a radical in any sense of the word, he was fully committed to his God and his family in that order.

Because of these affirmations of his fathers character the boy is certain that he, his baby sister, Clara Voncil, and little brother Bob, were all baptized as infants, into the family of faith in Christ Jesus. It is also reasonable to assume, these baptisms all took place at the First Methodist Church of Goodland, Kansas.

Even though father was a Lay Pastor, it is unlikely that he would baptize his own children. Also since Methodism is a "Catholic" faith, that is Catholic with an asteric *, these actions were considered baptisms and not simply christenings.[1]

"Baptism is a celebration of God's grace, not of human achievement. It is a means of grace through which God acts to seal the promises of the Gospel."[2]

"From the beginning, God graciously has included our children in His covenant. All God's promises are for them as well as for us. (Adults)

We are to teach them that they have been set apart by baptism as God's own children so that as they grow older they may respond to Him in personal faith and commitment.[3]

I realize that there are many who would argue this point ad nauseam but dear reader this is a recollection of a life not a dissertation on various theologies.

---

[1] Catholic* is the designation used in all Methodist, now United Methodist, materials to call attention to the Methodist understanding of the word Catholic as the original Latin definition of "Universal" and not Roman or Eastern Orthodox Catholic.

[2] The Worship Source Book, 2004 CRC Publications, Section Six, Baptism page 249.

[3] The Worship Source Book, 2004 CRC Publications, Section Six, Baptism page 258. Some capitalization and emphasis added by this author.

Now as the boy is in the winter of his years and looks back he is well aware of the presence of the promised "Guide" or "God" if you will, always there from the beginnings of memory, guiding, protecting as promised. Even throughout the year of his mid teens into his late thirties, when through the stubbornness and arrogance of youth and young adulthood, the boy refused to acknowledge the existence or even the veracity of this faithful Guide/God. He was always there as is evidenced in the hindsight of adult hood. The problem was that due to the circumstance of his life, there was no one there to teach him that he was God's child. Even that there was a God who loved him and walked by his side as companion and witness throughout his entire life.

RELIGION

The boys first memory of religion occurred in the spring of 1948 just prior to mother returning to Kansas to gather up her children and wisk them off to California.

The boy and two of his school chums decided that immediately upon the end of school they were going to go camping out on the Kansas prairie just like the cowboys did. They had it all planned. You know as only seven and eight year old boys can do. No tents, just bedrolls, cast iron skillet, bacon, eggs, coffee, etc etc. Actually they were going to camp in the pasture behind the barn at the family farm of one of the boys, but they were going to do it just like the cowboys.

When the boy announced these plans to his Uncle, his fathers brother and the grandma, he was told in no uncertain terms this was not going to happen. He instead was going to Vacation Bible School at the first Methodist Church starting on Monday immediately after the end of school for that year. All of this sounded like an oxymoron to the boy, (a big adult word, but one he would have used if he'd known about it,) after all if its school, its most certainly not vacation!

However, on Monday morning he found himself firmly ensconced in vacation bible school drawing pictures of weird stuff on paper plates with Crayolas. Not a good first encounter with religion. After, all how does drawing pictures on paper plates compare to camping out just like the cowboys? Other than that, there is only one memory of that one and only vacation Bible school and it is relatively positive in nature for two reasons.

First it was movies!

Second, it was movies supposedly taken by Missionaries in India. There were people dressed funny and all running around, either chasing or running from large snakes. It was a lot of fun. The boy laughed until his sides hurt. It was almost as good as camping out like the cowboys.

◦∞◦

The boy's next memories of religion cover a period of five or so years and are no positives at all.

About a year after the boys arrived in Idaho for the long stay their grandparents, (the boy has always thought to be a very strange name for this particular group of relatives. His experience has shown that there is in general, and in most individual cases, nothing at all "grand" about this particular group of people), he discovered they were very religious people. Never mind that they had not darkened the door of a church for at least thirty years, but they nevertheless returned to their church, becoming zealots in order to make up for the lost time. At least that is the way it seemed and indeed worked out in the lives of the boys.

From the morning of the first Sunday the whole family was pushed through the door of the small little church building on the west side of Nampa, life was never the same for the boys. Life with mothers parents was never pleasant, easy or even enjoyable, but now they were thrust into a building full of finger pointing people who were always trying to get the boys saved and baptized.

Since mothers parents became so zealous and were always trying to make up for lost time this happened to the boys, as the saying goes, every time the church doors opened. Indeed this was the case, for if there was any kind of meeting going on whenever, all of the work was done early and everyone was loaded up into the pickup truck and off to church they went.

Since there was only the farm Chevy pickup for transportation everyone was loaded up into it. There was another of the bug women, an aunt, still at home, so grandpa, the bug woman, and grandma all squeezed into the cab of the truck. The boys all rode in the open bed of the truck. Rain, shine, hail sleet, snow, or cold the three boys always rode the six or seven miles to church in the back. Spring, summer, fall and winter, there they were in the back of the truck.

This alone was enough to make religion unattractive, but then it didn't matter were the boys were going or if it was only grandpa and one of the boys going some where they always had to ride in the open bed of the truck. Therefore, this alone was enough for the notion of church of any kind, to curdle in the minds and hearts of the boys. Yet, also there was the constant pressure to get saved and baptized or else syndrome. That was a constant and at times forceful pressure on the part of the entirety of the congregation of that small little church whose denomination shall remain unnamed.

In later years all three of the boys made their peace with "God", but none to this day has ever darkened the door of a church of that denomination and never will. This determination was and is so strong, the boy has never read one of the many books written by a very well known and respected author, who is a leader in this denomination.

On the surface this was not a good introduction to religion by any reasonable definition. However, as the boy grew and at time encountered various aspects of religion as exhibited by other denominations and those presenting themselves as Christians, the boy found that this was pretty much the norm for religion. The result was that the boy actively avoided any and everything to do with any form of religion until his fortieth year. What A Waste!

During the 30 odd years that followed this second encounter there were other times when religion attempted to rear it's head in the boys life, but he immediately cut the head off the snake, so to speak and essentially was not bothered. Like Frank Sinatra, he "did it my way."

The boy's third encounter occurred in August of 1979 just a few short weeks after his thirty ninth birthday. To say it was an encounter with religion is not technically true as he now understands, but yet most of the civilized world would call it a religious experience. So we will leave it at that for now and see if the story as it unfolds can explain the difference.

The Boy had recently returned form a trip into Alberta Canada where he delivered three American Quarter Horses to a rancher who had purchased them from a friend of his in Oklahoma as breeding stock. It had been a long and enjoyable trip across the country with one of his daughters, who was in her late teens, accompanying him. They had been separated for some time by divorce from her mother and distance, so they made an epic trip out of it, passing through and exploring as much of both the United States and Canadian country side as they could, in the end both wishing to some degree that the trip didn't have to end.

The boy had passed his thirty ninth birthday while they were on the road. They celebrated that evening by going to dinner and a movie in West Yellowstone, Montana. They slept that night in the horse trailer in a parking lot because there were no hotel rooms available, it being late July and the middle of the tourist season. However, the raised goose neck portion of the trailer made a great place to rest on that warm summers night. The next day the boy and his daughter toured the sites of Yellowstone park then continuing on to Oklahoma and there reality of life.

For some reason during this trip the boys current wife had found reason to be disgruntled while the boy was on this trip and immediately upon his return home life was not a pleasant thing. The exact reasons are lost in time to a selective memory, that is a memory that has chosen to forget the unpleasantness which occurred. He does remember that money had a part in the problem. The trip to Canada while profitable, was not entirely as profitable as it would have been had the boy simply gone by himself, there and back, roughing it on the way.

However, to this day regardless of the eventual consequences, he does not regret one small second of the journey.

A BRIEF PAUSE

On the reverse cover of my previous book[4] the brief biography states,

"Ranch Hand, Farm Hand, Laborer, Veteran US Air Force, Ships Captain, Pastor, Brother in the Order of Saint Luke, Motorcycle Chaplain, not a Doctor, Lawyer, or Indian Chief.

B.S. University of Oklahoma, Master of Divinity, Chandler School of theology Emory University, Dr. of M6inistry, Kings Seminary Van Nuys Calif."

All of this is true I have done all of this and more. Yet why is this important for the reader to know? It is important because it is the context of a life lived simply, in similarity, to that of the reader. It is my hope that in the sharing of the memories of my life, the reader will realize the importance of their own story and the memories created in the living of it.

Also it is my hope that the reader will also become aware of the presence of the "Other" in the whole of their memories, just I did upon my awakening to this "Other's" presence in my life, during the fall of 1979. A companion who's presence, as I awakened, I realized was present in every memory in every corner of my life from the very beginning. Even before the beginning if that can be conceived. I have now through the years come to know this companion intimately. My companion is known throughout human

---

[4] I Ain't in Kansas No More!, This Can't Be God…. It Feels Too Real!! The Ewings Publishing copy right 2023

history and today by many different names. However, I call the "Other" or my companion, in these pages the "Guide". I also assign a male gender to my companion. I do so knowing full-well that He is gender-less and I do so for two reasons.

First, I am of a generation who is not caught up in the war over gender. Also for those of my generation it is familiar and ingrained to use the male gender when referring to my life companion.

Secondly, my companion during His tenure on this earth was male. He referred to the "Other" as "Father" thus assigning the male gender, and as I so famously told my Theology Examination Board Chairman, "If it is good enough for Him, it is good enough for me."

However, before I converse further concerning my companion there are more memories to share,

THE GUIDE

Up to this point I have avoided mention of The Guide mentioned in the preface. I have done this for the following reasons.

First, until this point in the recollections of our protagonist, The Guide or "God" has made no know appearances or outward revelations of His existence in the memories thus far. As far as the boy was concerned up to this point he had done it on his own without any assistance from any outside source.

As Dr. Phil would say, "How's that working out for you?"

Secondly, as I hope the recounting of the memories carried by the boy will help others to come to terms with their own life stories and memories, I have avoided the use of the "God" word. Because, I am aware, that upon its very revelation, there are those among the readers who will simply turn off the remainder of the story, even though it might be to their detriment.

However, the time has come to take the risk and begin to converse about the Sacred, or "God".

AUGUST 19, 1979

The boy had been home from the journey a little over two weeks. Two weeks marked by constant confrontation at home and small success in his business as a supplier of horse ranch equipment and supplies.

On that morning he had managed to get through breakfast, see his wife off to her job and taking their young daughter to her daycare.

After dropping of his daughter, knowing he was not well, went straight to his doctors office. The doctor made a quick examination and immediately called an ambulance and had him transported to the nearest hospital.

After a few hours of tests and all the stuff they do to you at a hospital under those circumstances, the boy was admitted and shortly found himself in a hospital gown, in a semi-dark room, in abject misery.

The doctor came in and told him, in his best bedside manner, that they weren't sure exactly what was wrong, but they were doing everything they could and hoped he would make it through the night, and that he would be closely monitored. (small country hospital.)

He called his wife at her job, telling her where he was, and that it appeared he was not going to be released in time to pickup their daughter from daycare. After a few well chosen words were exchanged he was informed she would take care of it. A few hours later a very angry woman, his wife, appeared in his room asking just what the H*** was going on and why the H*** was he in the hospital. After the explanations were made and a nurse was called to explain the medical side of things, his wife said these words. "Well you need to know that I've had it. If and when you ever get out of this place, I won't be there and neither will Mandy, (the daughter).

OK, fine I'll call the neighbor to make sure the stock, (horses, steers, chickens, rabbits, even a goat or two), is looked after until I get out., he replied.

She turned and exited the room without another sound.

So there he was alone in a hospital room with God only knew what was wrong with him, the doctor hoping he would make it through the night, and a wife who in the middle of all this had just walked out on him and their marriage. God what a mess he had made of his thirty nine years on this planet.

He laid down in the bed in that hospital room and quit. Gave up. No one that he knew gave a good G-- D—n, and neither did he any longer.

The next several hours are still to this day a blank. He was aware of the nurses constantly coming in doing what nurses do, but he didn't care. At this point he was simply waiting for whatever would happen, when he didn't make it through the night.

Slowly he became aware of a stranger in the room. A man, unknown to him, was sitting in the chair next to his bed. This man was telling him about someone he needed to meet. Someone named Jesus. The boy had heard all about this Jesus most of his life and frankly, because of that he didn't want anything to do with anything connected to this Jesus. In no uncertain terms and with as forceful a voice as he could muster, he told this stranger exactly what he could door with his Jesus, and told him to get out of the room or else. Or else what he had no idea. He never had any reason to find out, because the man promptly stood up and departed the room. The boy relaxed back on to his bed and into his misery, drifting off into nothingness.

At 10:30 pm, the boy knows it was 10:30pm because of a clock on the wall across from the foot of the bed. At that moment as registered by the clock on the wall, here began a cry coming from the depths of his misery, failures and worthlessness. The cry started more as an awareness that he was still alive then anything else, then just boiled up and out of him with these words,

> **"God if you are real, please help me!"**

The boy did not know where that had came from, but he knew it was his voice and his cry.

Instantly, a light switched on inside his body. It was like a hot glowing wire that ran from the top of his head to his groin, where it split into two branches and ran to the soles of his feet. The wire grew brighter and brighter until his entire being was filled in totality with its light and warmth. Some how he knew his cry had been heard. For the first time that day and truly for many years, he was relaxed. He no longer felt hopeless. He simply went to sleep.

He awoke several hours later. It was daylight. A bright sun filled the Oklahoma day. It was morning, the day was beginning for the hospital and those who were within its walls. Breakfast was brought in, nurses arrived, tests were made, blood samples were taken, all the activities you would expect.

He was a total basket case.

He knew something had happened! What? He had no idea.

He remembered the events of the evening before, but just what had taken place he didn't have a clue. All he knew was he had to get out of that place. He had to set about salvaging his life, or attempting to at least.

The first strange event of the day happened when he asked the nurse if she knew who the man was who had been in his room, because he needed to apologize to him. He was told there had been no one in his room. She had been on duty all night and there had been no visitors on the floor all night.

The second strange was when the doctor arrived shortly before noon with the news, "We can't find anything wrong with you! Whatever it was that brought you in here yesterday is gone. You can go home as soon as the nurses get the release papers written up. Don't know what happened to you yesterday, but today your as healthy as one of your horses!"

Shortly thereafter he found himself walking out the front door into the parking lot towards his truck. HE WAS ABSOLUTELY A RAVING BASKET CASE at this point.

He was alone! All His life he had been alone. Always striving to belong to someone or something. However, here he was at the ripe old age of thirty nine and he was alone. No Job. No Wife. Three children who would not be caught dead in the same town with him, let alone in his company. He had a six year old daughter who thought he hung the moon and the stars, but, he knew from painful experience, that by the time the dust settled she also would join the ranks of those who couldn't stand him.

All his life he had lived the motto of the Frank Sinatra song and as the lyric says, "I did it my Way!" Largely because he had been forced to do it that way to survive and what had it gotten him. Nothing!!

Yet, here he was suddenly confronted with the very real knowledge and certainty that he had never ever been alone, he had simply been to stubborn, deaf, dumb, and blind to see the life long companion and guide who had been by his side all along. Now he had met this companion and witness, yet there was still no one to teach him the truth of this life long Guide.

So now what was he to do?

The answer to that question as Paul Harvey used to say "is the rest of the story."

The rest of the story has taken some forty three years to unveil. Those years and the lessons learned are the drive behind this writing. The first thing that happened was that our Hero was confronted full force with the life strangling force of Religion in its late twentieth century Christian incarnation. The boy was confronted full force by twentieth century religion in its evangelical christian format as practiced in the Buckle of the Bible Belt of the United states of America.

I have included here a definition of Religion taken from the Encyclopedia Britannica. There are many others in nameless dictionaries, however, while worded differently they all state the same thing in their endless differences of language and nuance. Please read it closely and you will find that religion is essentially whatever the individual or an individual group of people decide it is.

> *Religion, <u>human</u> beings' relation to that which they regard as holy, sacred, absolute, spiritual, divine, or worthy of especial reverence. It is also commonly regarded as consisting of the way people deal with ultimate concerns about their lives and their fate after <u>death</u>. In many traditions, this relation and these concerns are expressed in terms of one's relationship with or attitude toward gods or spirits; in more <u>humanistic</u> or <u>naturalistic</u> forms of religion, they are expressed in terms of one's relationship with or attitudes toward the broader human community or the natural world. In many religions, texts are deemed to have scriptural status, and people are esteemed to be invested with spiritual or moral authority. Believers and worshipers participate in and are often enjoined to perform devotional or contemplative practices such as <u>prayer</u>, <u>meditation</u>, or particular <u>rituals</u>. <u>Worship</u>, moral conduct, right <u>belief</u>, and participation in religious institutions are among the constituent elements of the religious life.*[5]

It was this that confronted our Protagonist as he emerged from the hospital, fresh, clean and confused. All he knew for certain was

---

[5] Britannica, The Editors of Encyclopaedia. "religion". *Encyclopedia Britannica*, 19 Oct. 2023, https://www.britannica.com/topic/religion. Accessed 10 December 2023.

he needed to find someone who could tell him the truth concerning his experience and about the Deity or Spirit that had so strangely warmed his heart and apparently cleansed his soul in the process.

He had heard all the current, at the time, teachings from all the television preachers etc. After all he lived in the buckle of the Bible Belt. He was surrounded by the culture of the religious teaching that flowed from the fountains in Tulsa. No one who lived in the United States of America in 1979 could not honestly say they had never heard of Jesus, sin and Salvation.

However, the honest truth is that there existed and continues to exist, a great number of people who remain more confused than enlightened. More determined to ignore rather than hear, and our worthy hero most defiantly belonged to that group.

Please do understand, the boy is most grateful for the path he took, even though it was and is a two edge sword of sorts. But I am ahead of the story.

The boy only knew that something extraordinary had happened to him and he needed to know what it was and what to do.

In the vernacular of his world "God" had answered his request. He had indeed witnessed to him that he was real and had helped him. However, there was a strangeness about the "help". His life was still a mess. His wife and daughter were not there. He still had no income. Yet, he knew there was a change. No one could have experienced what he had and pretend there had not been a change. But What was it?

He woke on the first Sunday morning, just two days after leaving the hospital, with the sure and certain knowledge that he need to go to church. Church would be where he would find the answers. After all church is where "God" lived. Church is where there would be people who could tell him about what had happened and help him put his life back together. There in lies the two edged sword!

LIFE ON THE EDGE OF A TWO EDGED SWORD

The two edges are there because of that which is taught and commonly practiced, and that which is the actuality of the presence of the Guide in ones life. As it turns out this is also the most difficult portion of these memories to process into written words.

That first Sunday morning after leaving the hospital the boy arrived in the parking lot of Metro Church in Edmond, Oklahoma rather early. In fact the parking lot was empty. This didn't matter to our protagonist, because he was busily involved in a one way argument with whoever it was that had met him in the hospital room a few nights earlier. He was still attempting to determine just what had happened and just what he was supposed to do. Our hero is not the most patient of individuals.

Eventually the parking lot began to fill. The people walking by looked at him, smiling as they passed by his truck. A few probably even wondered who that strange person was sitting in his truck talking to himself.

Finally he determined where to enter the church by following others into the building. He was welcomed, ushered to a seat at the end of a pew where he looked around at the large auditorium. There were a lot of people standing in groups, talking to each other. Calling out to someone as they entered the room. All in all it was a rather noisy place filled to the brim with smiling, laughing people. It was a place were even though he did not know one soul, he felt safe and the frantic nervousness he had felt since his experience at the hospital left him. He was calm.

A lot of things happened rather quickly that morning. A group of people approached him, introduced themselves and asked him all sorts of questions. Where did he live? Where did he work? Etc etc. Eventually he was introduced to a man and his wife, Ed, and Ruth Green. This couple and our boy quickly became close fast friends. Ruth particularly guided and helped the boy through the process of understanding his encounter with the divine and his finding a place at Metro Church.

They also were there to help pick up the pieces when our fledgling believer slipped and the sharp edge of the two edged sword cut him into pieces. Each time Ruth and Ed would simply gather him up and by simply loving him as a brother, sew him back together once more.

You see The Christian Religion as it is practiced is a religion of "Do not's". All while expressing "anything is possible for those who believe."

Anything is possible, but first you must live a perfect life to achieve the possible. As soon as our boy's story was told within the church community there were many who came to him and their massage was most always something like this, "You have been singled out by God as special for some reason. Because of this you must be an example of the pure life in Christ for all of us. We are so blessed to have you here!" One edge of the sword.

Then when our fledgling believer stumbled, which was often, the message was something like this, "You can't be of God and have something like this happen in your life. We don't know what happened to you, but it couldn't have been God, if this is the way your falling short of the mark!" The other edge of the sword.

Our young friend was continually on the edge of that sword. The interesting part is that none of the religious teaching gathered from various parts of the church world ever seemed to coincide with the entity he knew and grew to love so strongly over the years. This entity is the Third edge of the sword. The edge which cuts away all else while healing all the cuts of the other two edges.

Confusing ain't it?

In this friend he found none of the restrictions only promise and hope. He never has found any condemnation or even reproof when he has fallen short of the example, only an outstretched hand waiting to pick him up in order to begin again.

Religion from the church world and even while in seminary, always is condemning and requiring sacrifice, subjugation and even death as the only means or pathway to the promise and hope our boy finds continually offered to him by his Guide.

There, have been many churches attended in the forty four or so years since our boy met his "God" and Friend in that hospital room on August 19, 1979, and many things have been learned. Few of them have been learned in "Church."

Probably the most important item learned is that none of us is ever alone!

If you have read this story you are aware of the fact that in the view point of the corporal world our protagonist grew up and lived his life mostly alone. However, the truth is he was never alone! The God of his and of all creation was and is continuously beside him walking the same path. Whispering in his ear the way to go, all that is required is the acknowledgment of HIS presence and a willing ear to listen.

Our boy's Guide and friend is also, Your Guide and Friend. There is no complicated process or system of prayer or subjugation required to know Him, He knows you and is there beside you. For you also and for everyone all that is required is accepting His presence, and listening with a willing ear,(heart).

There is no two edged sword in this Friend and Guide. There is only acceptance and love, regardless of any circumstance or condition. The two edged sword is the weapon wielded by religion, when humanity imposes it's will, as supreme, over that which is divine and pure.

The two edge sword of this Guide and Friend is simply this. Love others as you love Him, *one edge*. Gather together in community with all his creation to better share His love with all who have need, *the other edge*.

The request of the boy now in the winter of his years, and because of the experience gained from those years is to ask the reader to put away religion and simply take a walk through life with the perfection and love who is now and has been forever by your side, and share that love as He shares it with you.

I wish to make what I am trying to say plain and clear.

Christ Jesus died once and was resurrected once for **ALL.**

*God our Savior,... who desires everyone to be saved and to come to the knowledge of the truth. For there is one God; there is also one mediator between God and humankind, Christ Jesus, himself human, who gave himself a ransom for **all**...* **1 Timothy 2:3-6a NRSV emphasis added**

That means everyone. The Holy Spirit remains here with us. Christ through the presence of the Holy Spirit walks beside each of us from the moment of our birth. He is constantly speaking to us, telling us of his love for us, and giving us directions and information concerning His plan for our lives. He is always there beside us, guiding and pleading with us to follow Him and His advice.

It is up to us to recognize His voice and accept Him.

All of us are "saved"!

That work was done once and for all on the cross at Calvary. Our task is simply to accept that, and live our lives according to the examples He has given us.

The text below delineates everything He requires of us. Nothing more is ever required in His words passed down to us through the scriptures. Read the text closely, for if you do, you will discover the Guide who has been by your side for your entire life. He is your Guide! He is there only for you and the life he guides you toward is totally unique. He is there for all of His creation yet He wishes to guide everyone, and guides everyone who will listen through their own uniqueness which has been ordained from the foundations of the universe. All you have to do is listen and choose HIM. There is no one size fits all. Everyone is unique.

Listen closely and you will discover the most exciting life you can imagine as you walk with Him beside you.

"When the Son of Man comes in his glory, and all the angels with him, then he will sit on the throne of his glory. All the nations will be gathered before him, and he will separate people one from another as a shepherd separates the sheep from the goats, and he will put the sheep at his right hand and the goats at the left. Then the king will say to those at his right hand, "Come, you that are blessed by my Father, inherit the kingdom prepared for you from the foundation of the world; for **I was hungry and you gave me food, I was thirsty and you gave me something to drink, I was a stranger and you welcomed me, I was naked and you gave me clothing, I was sick and you took care of me, I was in prison and you visited me.'**

Then the righteous will answer him, "Lord, when was it that we saw you hungry and gave you food, or thirsty and gave you something to drink? And when was it that we saw you a stranger and welcomed you, or naked and gave you clothing? And when was it that we saw you sick or in prison and visited you?' And the king will answer them, "Truly I tell you, just as you did it to one of the least of these who are members of my family, you did it to me.' Then he will say to those at his left hand, "You that are accursed, depart from me into the eternal fire prepared for the devil and his angels;

for I was hungry and you gave me no food, I was thirsty and you gave me nothing to drink,

I was a stranger and you did not welcome me, naked and you did not give me clothing, sick and in prison and you did not visit me.'

Then they also will answer, "Lord, when was it that we saw you hungry or thirsty or a stranger or naked or sick or in prison, and did not take care of you?'

Then he will answer them, "Truly I tell you, just as you did not do it to one of the least of these, you did not do it to me.' And these will go away into eternal punishment, but the righteous into eternal life." **Matthew 25:25-46 NRSV emphasis added**

PART IV

The Rest of the Story
A FINAL WORD

AUGUST, 1,1984

Deborah Ann Pollard married our boy. The wedding was held in the club house of the apartment house complex where the boy lived at the moment. It was held there because the church as the religious entity it was, would not allow the wedding to take place on its hollowed grounds, because of the boy's past marital history. Religion had determined, it just could not sanction the union.

The ceremony however, was conducted by two ministers associated with the church. Strange indeed.

The story of Debbie, as she is known, is told in another volume untitled "I Ain't in Kansas No More"[6], so it won't be retold here.

Friend's of the couple, at the time of the marriage, declared strongly and often, that it would not last. Who knows? They may be correct. It has only been a little over thirty nine years now and its not over yet. Anything could happen.

To quote Debbie, "I may not be the first or even the second but I hold the record."

I as the author, and the second half of this union, am required by all good consciousness to state here and now my life has forever been the better because of Debbie. However, she most certainly has deserved more than she has received. She certainly got the short end of the stick, as the saying goes.

That is when she married me, she deserved better than she got!

---

[6] I Aint in Kansas No More! See foot note #4 for further information.

Deborah

IT'S NOT OVER YET

www.ingramcontent.com/pod-product-compliance
Lightning Source LLC
LaVergne TN
LVHW041949070526
838199LV00051BA/2958